EDGE OF SIN

LAUREN BIEL

Library of Congress Cataloging-in-Publication Data

Edge of Sin/Lauren Biel 1st ed.

Printed in the United States of America

Cover Design: Pretty in Ink Creations

Content Editing: Sugar Free Editing

Interior Design: Sugar Free Editing

For more information on this book and the author, visit: www.LaurenBiel.com

Please visit LaurenBiel.com for a full list of content warnings.

*This book is dedicated to the women who spit on red flags
when it comes to their book boyfriends*

Chapter One

Gia

I halted for a moment to admire a beautiful white hydrangea past the front door's archway. The men lowered their guns as my hips swayed past each of them, their eyes locked on my body, burning through me. *They need some less impressionable guards.* My heels tapped against the tile floors with confident steps that ensured no one stopped me on my way into the huge home on the hill. The steel door slammed shut behind me, and the sound echoed through the enormous, empty hallway. No one defended the halls, including the one leading toward the library where I would inevitably face fierce opposition. The moment they saw me, not even my body could get me out of the situation I was putting myself in.

My hands trembled, and I took a deep breath to settle my nerves before opening the heavy wooden door. I willed the shaking to stop so I could appear more confident than I felt. *You can't show weakness,* I reminded myself.

The moment the door closed behind me, every gun

raised from the men's hips, which I expected. The metallic sounds of racking rifles and pistols rose toward the vaulted ceilings in the open room. The scent of lemon lingered there, as if the housekeeper doused the room with cleaning products. I curled my lip at the strong aroma and lifted my hands to show that I came unarmed . . . mostly.

I scanned the room. Five large men dressed in suits had their weapons drawn on me, a small spitfire of a woman, but an enemy, nonetheless.

"Why are you here, Miss Silvani?" a gruff voice said from a tall office chair with its back toward me. The man swiveled to face me, his dark eyes scanning me up and down. His gaze hovered at my chest, which was accentuated by my tight black dress. Behind him, pictures of his family decorated the wall, each man wearing his suit better than the last generation. Gold rings wrapped around all their fingers as they held them in front of their laps.

"You can call me Gia." I rubbed my sweaty palms down my dress.

"And you can call me Mr. Viglione. We're not on informal terms, *Miss Silvani*," he said with an emphasis on my name.

"That's fine." The guns remained trained on me with every step I took toward the boss, and not even the exaggerated wiggle of my hips could encourage them to drop their weapons. "I have a proposition for you, sir." I looked around the room at the men. "Can your goons at least lower their guns? I'm very clearly unarmed." Flirtation laced my words as I ran my hands down my curves.

His lips pulled into a disappointed frown when I showed no fear of the guns. That's what happened when you grew up in the home of the most prominent mafia family. I didn't bat an eye when a gun was drawn on me, not even when it was five of them. That was nothing new and certainly not out of the ordinary. My family would be the same way, although a Viglione wouldn't have made it to this point in our residence. The only thing out of the ordinary was my presence in the home of the second most prominent family.

The family always chasing after my father.

"I know where the dolls in your family hide their weapons." Mr. Viglione gestured toward one of his men. The man holstered his pistol, stepped forward, and ran his rough hands up my dress. He pulled out a small pistol concealed on my thigh. *Damn it.* Laughter filled the room as the man retreated with my only source of protection in a house full of animals.

The Vigliones were a cruel family, building their empire on fear and retaliation. My family wasn't perfect, but at least we had hearts. Everything about this situation felt like a red flag, but in typical fashion, I spit on red flags.

"Can we talk now?" I asked, a hint of annoyance rearing its head in my tone.

"What could you possibly have to talk about? You're lucky I didn't kill you the moment you stepped foot in my home. You got a pair of balls on you, I'll give ya that." Mr. Viglione nodded as he lit a cigar, the smoke hiding his dark, soulless eyes. His cheeks puffed as he inhaled the smoke.

I stepped toward him, and his guards met my steps and closed in on me. Silvio waved them away, and they returned to their positions along the wall, their watchful eyes still on me. A smile crept across my face as I crossed the soft carpet in front of his desk, the material muffling the sound of my heels. I leaned over, grabbed his cigar, and placed it between my painted lips, puffing on the smoke. A power move.

"I would like to be abducted," I said as I handed the cigar back to him.

His mouth dropped open. "You would like to be what?" He extinguished the tip in a golden ashtray.

"You heard me. I'd like to stage my abduction." I bent over the large wooden desk, running my hand along the grain. My breasts pulled together directly in Silvio's line of vision. He only looked away once I made my request.

"I'm not interested in getting into a war with your family, Gia," he said with a dismissive wave of his hand. "For the first time in forty-five years, we're amicable."

"I thought we weren't on informal terms, Silvio." My lips spread into a slow, sensual smile. "Nonetheless, not even for a hundred million?"

Silvio's squinty eyes widened as much as his fat cheeks would allow. "Explain."

Money always swayed us. That's where the morals of our families overlapped.

"We'll attach a hefty ransom bill of a hundred million, but I need your family to help me do it."

"I don't think you know what you're asking." He released a devilish smile. "Besides, I'm not putting our families at war again to give your hot little ass a hundred mil."

The room filled with laughter.

"I'm asking for thirty percent, that's all." My lips pouted as I stared at him.

Silvio raised his hand, and the laughter stopped. "Let me get this straight. You want us to abduct you, hold you for ransom, and pay you a portion of the money?" He rubbed a hand through his black beard, as dark as the hair on his head.

"Yes. I'm handing you an easy target with a sizable payout for minimal effort."

Silvio picked up the cigar, shifted it between his fingers, and tightened his lips. "Deal, but this ain't going to be no walk in the park for you, not in my home." His voice deepened with the threat. He reached into a drawer and pulled out a burner phone, sliding it along the table toward me. "We'll be in touch." With that, he pointed the cigar at me, dismissing me with a wave of his hand.

Enzo

"WHY ARE you even considering this, Pops?" I sat in the chair beside him in the big lounge area. Silvio's overbearing desk accommodated his large stature, a physique none of us wanted to inherit—fat cheeks that made his eyes appear small and beady, thin lips that always made him look unhappy, and a gut hidden behind his expensive custom jacket.

"She's a compelling one," Silvio said with a motion of his hands to mimic Gia's curves. He laughed as he plucked his smoking cigar from the ashtray.

"That may be, but why would we want a rift between the families after we finally settled things between us?"

"Nothing is ever truly settled, son. Stagnancy just means no advancement." Silvio puffed on his cigar, letting the rich aroma fill the air in a visible cloud.

"But why her? You know she ain't no peach," I tried to reason with him. I absolutely despised the Silvani family as much as the next guy, but that damn Giovanna was something else entirely. She was fiery, impossible to talk to, and had no issue with taking revenge. She was such a cold-hearted bitch, which was why she was the perfect woman in a business like this. The fact that she was stunning didn't help the matter none, either.

"Consider it an investment. Seventy mil is a sizable payout for babysitting the broad for a few days."

"Well, don't say I didn't warn you when shit hits the fan. This ain't going to be the easy gig you think it will be."

"That's why I'm putting you in charge of this whole thing." Silvio gestured toward me. He smirked as he unbuttoned his jacket, exposing the strained white dress shirt tucked into his dress pants.

"Whoa, no, this is *your* bright fucking idea, Pops." I rose to my feet and leaned over the desk, my face inches from his. "I want nothing to do with this." My words were fire, and I meant for them to burn that idea to the ground.

"If that's what you want, Enzo, just know you'd have been a lot nicer to her than I will be. Go on." He waved me away.

I opened my mouth to speak, but the words tangled together in my throat. My shoes echoed on the tile floor as I stomped toward the door, but my hand hovered on the handle.

"Fine, I'll take care of her," I said with a frustrated breath as I left the room, slamming the door behind me.

Chapter Two

Gia

"We lost how much money?" My father's voice boomed through the library, rattling the picture frames on the wall. He slammed his fist on the table, sounding almost like a gunshot—something we were all too familiar with. I knew what gunshots sounded like before I knew how to write my name.

I stood just outside the door, pictures of a smiling family staring back at me. My father's arm was wrapped around my mother's, leaning over me and my brothers. Everyone was dressed in colorful Hawaiian shirts, a stark contrast to the family photos at the Vigliones'. We were a happier family. Well, we were at one time. I felt a pang of sadness as I looked at my eldest brother's short, dark hair. He wore a smile that women killed for. I missed the hell out of him and losing him was one of several nails in the coffin holding my desire to remain in the business. It also didn't help that our closest allies had gone down. Most ended up in prison, broke, or both. It was only a matter of time before they came for our family.

"No, that's fucking great! Thanks anyway!" my father shouted into his cell phone, creating a sinking feeling in my chest. He threw his phone to the ground and gripped the arms of the chair.

"Daddy, what's wrong?" I asked as I walked past the wall of books in my bare feet, rubbing my hand along the leather spines. Soft classical music played from a stereo in the corner of the room, though it didn't cut through the tension. I felt as if I were suffocating, and I took a deep breath as I stepped toward him.

He looked up at me, trying to fake a smile. "Oh, hello, darling." His hand wiped down his face, leaving a deflated smirk in its wake.

"What happened?"

"Nothing you need to worry your pretty little head about. Where's your mother?" The fireplace flickered and cast a shadow on his face, accentuating the high cheekbones I'd inherited from him.

"She went up to bed. Stop deflecting. What happened?" I sat in the chair beside him, the flames dancing in front of me. The fire engulfed the logs, leaving blackened destruction in its path.

He groaned. "One of our parlors got shut down, and all the money from there is gone."

"How much?"

"Ten million," he said with a sigh as he brushed his hand through his hair.

"Ouch." I played with the fabric of my pajama pants, avoiding his gaze. Guilt began to gnaw at me. *The feds are getting closer and closer.*

My family wanted nothing to do with the drug trade.

My father had no interest in being a kingpin. He was a crime boss, and a damn good one. He preferred to deal with illegal gambling, racketeering, and money laundering. We flew under the radar by using offshore accounts, but we could feel the hot breath of the feds on us. They were closing in. If I had been an innocent member of my family, I would have stayed, but I had lain with the men and destroyed lives like the rest of them. I was a crime boss' daughter, and there was a certain level of responsibility that came with that distinction. My hands trembled just enough when I aimed my gun, so it was time to put it down.

"It's okay, baby girl. It doesn't break us. Your brother is going to take it harder than me."

"How so?"

"His best friend was one of the patrons at the parlor. When he saw police, he couldn't keep his itchy finger off the trigger. Killed a cop. He's done." My father exhaled and lifted his drink from the table—a golden liquid with ice cubes swimming around in the glass.

"Poor Ro."

My brother, Roberto, had big dreams for the business, though his small stature didn't make him intimidating enough. He swam in suits, always needing them to be taken in to accommodate his slight frame. Roberto was handsome and well-liked by the women in the families, but the businessmen spoke above and behind him instead of to him.

Ro appeared in the library's doorway. "What was all the yelling about?"

"Come here, kid." Our father gestured with his drink toward the chair beside him. Being summoned toward our father was rarely a good thing, and Ro's face showcased his concern.

"What's wrong?" he asked as he scanned our expressions. He brushed the long, dark hair out of his face as his lips tightened. "Tell me!"

"Fonz got arrested," our father said.

"That dumb bastard. For what?"

"Ro, he killed a cop," I said. I hated when bushes were beaten around.

Roberto's dark eyes rounded as the corners of his lips turned down. "What . . . why?" Ro turned and punched the wall. Nothing broke. He couldn't even create a dent.

I wiped the bridge of my nose beneath my glasses.

"The parlor got raided," our father said, "and well, you know Fonz."

"He's gone. He's a lifer." Ro sighed.

"Yup," our father said as he shook his glass. "Such is this life, Ro."

"We didn't ask for this, Dad!" Roberto paced the hardwood floors.

"You think I did? I was born into it just like you and your sister! You have responsibilities as a Silvani. I rebelled against the drug trade, said that I wanted nothing to do with that life after I saw what they did to the children of other families. Take out a family from the bottom, Ro. That's what they do." My dad stood, his tall frame towering over Roberto. "I tried to give you all a different life, a better empire to run once I'm gone!"

I crossed my legs and leaned onto my hip, twirling my black hair around my fingers. If you asked me at eighteen what I believed in, it would have been dreams of becoming a boss bitch. At twenty-five, I just wanted to leave the East Coast, maybe even the country. I wanted peace. There was no rest for the wicked here.

Chapter Three

Gia

I looked at the phone on the counter as I stepped out of the shower. The screen illuminated, showing no calls, and I groaned. *Come on, where are they?* My resolve was weakening, the guilt building with every passing day. *How hard is it to plan an abduction? Maybe they decided against it.* There was no way to contact the Vigliones, and they kept it that way on purpose. Sure, I could visit their home, but it was always a risk to show up at a rival family's sanctuary.

The cold porcelain made me shiver as I dried my long black hair. Soft curls nearly level with my chest framed the tan complexion I inherited from my mother. I painted my lips a deep maroon, accentuating my full lower lip, which always made me look pouty. My dark brown eyes nearly melded with my pupils. Unless someone got close enough to kiss me, they wouldn't be able to differentiate them. I was a black widow. Almost every man I had slept with ended up dead. Maybe it was my father's doing or maybe it was dumb luck, but I possessed a kiss of death. It had been years since

I let a man touch me, and I didn't plan on changing that any time soon.

A buzzing sound broke my concentration, and I looked at the vibrating phone on the counter. My hands went numb, and I almost couldn't answer the call. The phone beeped as I hit the green button. I lifted it to my ear and waited, hearing nothing but silence on the other line.

"Seven p.m., Gerusso's restaurant parking lot."

The call ended before I could respond, but the nauseating words replayed in my head as I looked at the phone and sighed at the clock. It was already after five. *Not very much time.*

I walked to my room, dressed myself in a low-cut black shirt and a pair of tight jeans, and began to pack a small bag. My palms dampened with every passing minute. *Am I really doing this?* A photo of my family guilted me from its place on my dresser, and I packed it away in my bag.

Enzo

MY EYES LOCKED on the black BMW pulling into the parking lot. I rubbed my hand through my beard as I watched her step out of the car and into the cool night air. Seeing her flooded my mind with memories of when I let myself be weak and miss a target. I remembered her standing in front of me, those deep, dark eyes staring back at me as the pistol trembled in her hand. She wasn't a killer yet, still naïve to that part of our lives. She fired the gun and the bullet whizzed past my head. My finger pulled the trigger in response, almost instinctively, but the slight rise in my barrel sent the bullet sailing above her head. Was it intentional? I don't know, but it was the only reason she was still alive, standing in front of me.

She drew a cigarette from a pack and put it between her lips. The lighter's flame kept blowing out, even when she covered it with her other hand. The wind played with her hair, and I took a deep breath as she looked toward my car.

"Sir, do you have a light?" she called toward me from across the parking lot.

I looked back at Lorenzo, and he offered me a sly smirk. *Too easy.* "Sure, yeah! Come on over," I yelled toward her, and she made her way across the parking lot, her hips swaying beneath her long jacket. The smoke billowed from the car as I lowered the window further.

"Smells like you have something better to smoke." She leaned on my door with a soft smile.

"Want some?" I pulled the roach from a small ashtray in my center console, took a deep drag, and handed it to her. She pulled the cigarette away from her mouth and tucked it behind her ear. I couldn't keep my eyes off her lips as she inhaled and blew the smoke into the air above her head. *Her lips are . . .* I shook my head.

Two of my fingers raised between the front seats, gesturing toward Lorenzo. He got out of the car, and Gia dropped the roach to the ground.

"I don't want any trouble." Her hand instinctively reached into her jacket to grab her pistol.

"Interesting, because you asked for exactly that." I smirked as Lorenzo wrapped his palm around her mouth and yanked her against his body.

Despite the large hand stifling her voice, she released a scream. The car beeped as I opened the door and stepped onto the pavement. As I taped her wrists behind her, her eyes glossed with welling tears, but she would never let them fall. That wasn't how Gia was.

I reached within the cold fabric of her coat to disarm her, my hand hovering on her hip. "You won't be needing that," I said as the pistol found a new home in the back of my waistband. Silver flashed in my hand as I pulled a roll of tape from the floorboard and ripped off a piece to put over her mouth. Her nostrils flared.

Lorenzo chuckled as he threw her into the backseat of the SUV. "You made this quite easy. We didn't even have to come to you."

I returned to the driver's seat, started the engine, and raised the tinted windows. No one could see inside. Only once we left the innards of the city did I gesture for Lorenzo to remove the tape. The moment it left her mouth, the car was filled with a flurry of curse words. Lorenzo moved to put the tape back over her mouth, but I lifted my hand.

"Let her get it out of her system."

I expected nothing less from Giovanna Silvani as I stared at her smudged lipstick and crazed eyes in the rearview mirror. She looked like an animal caught in a snare. Maybe she was.

"You motherfuckers! I would have come willingly! Now I'm just pissed right the fuck off!" She screamed and kicked at my seat.

"We don't half ass things in this family. I was told to abduct you, so I abducted you."

"Did they not tell you this is *staged*? It's fake!" Each word snapped at the end.

"I don't ask questions," I said with a shrug of my shoulders.

"Maybe you should start," she hissed as she struggled against the restraints on her wrists.

As we arrived at the end of the long driveway leading up to the house, Lorenzo placed the tape over her mouth again. I could still hear her yell, "Fuck you!" beneath the tape, and I couldn't help but smirk. Once I put the car in park, Lorenzo pulled Gia toward the end of the seat and threw her over his broad shoulders. She struggled against Lorenzo's grasp as his hand rose to caress her ass, and her mouth continued to release muffled noises that altered the night's quiet ambiance.

We carried her past the marbled halls and into a back bedroom. Lorenzo dropped her onto the bed, and I knelt in front of her as a look of recognition flashed on her face once she saw me in the light of the room. I was surprised she didn't recognize me sooner. Eyes this blue weren't common in our families. As she writhed against the restraints, I caressed her cheek before ripping the tape off in a quick motion.

"Fuck!" she shouted.

"I'm Enzo," I said as I pulled a knife from my belt and began to cut the tape from her slender wrists.

"I know who you are," she snapped.

"You remember me?"

"Now I do. You're lucky I wasn't a better shot back then." The tape broke open and she rubbed her wrists.

"Our families have been fighting since before we were born, and here you are, pitting us against your own at a time of peace." My gaze dropped as I brushed a hand through my dark hair.

"There's no peace between our families."

"You may think that way, but your father had reached out to us for business. We were nearly allies." A smile crept across my face. "That will all go to shit once he finds out what we did to his dear daughter." My hand brushed through her damp hair.

"Can we?" Lorenzo asked as he unzipped his fly.

I looked at her, then back at Lorenzo, hesitating as a dark thought spread its shadowy fingers through my mind. She'd feel incredible if I forced my way inside her.

And then she'll try to kill me. I rubbed my thumb along her lips. "As good as she looks like she'd feel, not tonight."

"But boss—"

"I said not tonight!" I rose to my feet and locked eyes with Lorenzo. "We're leaving."

Chapter Four

Gia

I stayed up most of the night, pacing with regret over my scheme. They had locked the door on their way out, trapping me in this bedroom. My mind raced, making it hard to do much more than worry about what I'd gotten myself into.

Still-life paintings encased in gold and silver frames covered the walls. The gold embroidery on the comforter gleamed in the gentle overheard light, and the plush bedding felt expensive. Soft sand-colored carpet cushioned my feet as I paced. Aside from how I got there—and being locked in—it wasn't a bad place to stay.

When I walked into the large en suite bathroom and looked at myself, my mouth dropped open. *Oh boy.* I turned the faucet's silver handle above the sink and rubbed a bar of floral-scented soap between my hands, scrubbing my face until every trace of my smeared makeup slithered down the drain. Satisfied, I forced myself to lie on the king-sized memory foam mattress and wrapped myself in the cozy blankets. The accommodations were incredible, but the hospitality in the room pissed me off. *Fuck you, Enzo.* The moment I'd seen him in the light, memories flashed to the front of my mind. And I hated him. It had been so damn long since I last saw him, and my brain had forced him out of my thoughts for all those years. For good reason.

I didn't think any of this through. I'd been too enamored by the freedom dangling in front of me.

My eyelids grew heavy, and I fought sleep until I gave in and let myself drift out of the nightmare I'd put myself in.

THE SUN SHINING through the large bay windows crept beneath my eyelids and forced me awake, despite my body still feeling like I needed more sleep. I yawned as I looked around and remembered where I was.

What did I do?

I got out of bed and went to the bathroom to clean up. When I walked back into the bedroom, there was a knock on the door, and it opened with a slow creak. The familiar gruff voice of Silvio broke the silence in the room.

"I take it your arrival here was to your liking?" He smirked as he tossed my bag into the room.

"You know damn well it wasn't."

"Well, shit, that's what I get for sending my son to do my job," he said with sarcasm lacing his words. His flirty stare hovered over the cleavage peeking from the top of my low-cut shirt. I covered my chest with my arms.

Enzo came into the room behind his father. He wore black dress pants and a dark blue dress shirt that paired well with his mesmerizing eyes.

Fuck that. I tore my gaze away from his face, looking anywhere else.

"We need to know you aren't concealing any weapons or wires," Silvio said with a grin. "Take your shirt and pants off."

Enzo's eyes snapped to his father as he wrung his hands together in front of his lap.

"We disarmed her last night," Enzo said, but Silvio waved him off.

I hesitated, knowing my family would do the same thing, just not in such a perverted manner. My breath hitched as I grabbed the bottom of my shirt and lifted it over my head, sending my hair tumbling down my back. My eyes remained on the men as I unzipped my jeans and wiggled them down until the fabric bunched at my knees. Silvio's eyes climbed my body. Enzo stared at me as well, his gaze lingering on the black bra pushing my cleavage together.

"Nope, no wires." Silvio groaned. His cellphone rang, and he looked at me with clear desire before leaving the room to do business.

I was alone with Enzo.

He walked toward me, each step more confident than the last. He reached around me and ran his hand along my spine until his fingertips met the waistband of my panties. I looked up at him, my thoughts racing and taking U-turns into sexual territory. *No fucking way. Fuck him.* His fingers dipped past my underwear and drew me out of my mind, a shiver climbing up every vertebra in my back. I blew out a breath and took a step back from him.

"Why?" I demanded.

"Why what, Giovanna?" His voice was soft and sultry, unlike how he'd spoken last night.

"Did you actually abduct me? I shouldn't have been taken like that. It wasn't part of the plan."

"We make the plans, not you." Despite his words rubbing me raw, his tone made my mind swim. Enzo rubbed a hand through his short beard as I gathered my faculties and grabbed a change of clothes from my bag. His gaze remained on me as I bent to pick up the bag, and I rolled my eyes so hard I thought they'd get stuck back there. "Did you really think we'd warmly welcome a rival family's daughter? I mean, this is kinder than Silvio wanted, so be thankful for that."

"Fuck you," I snapped as I put on a fresh pair of jeans.

"I should punish you for that mouth in my house, you know. I could silence you so easily by putting my cock in that bratty mouth of yours." His finger dragged along my mouth, the tip of his thumb tugging down my lower lip. "When I found out it was the Silvani girl, I knew I'd be dealing with the *worst* attitude." He brushed his hand across the small of my back. Shivers vibrated my body.

Fuck this guy.

"Anyway, I've been given the delightful job of sitting with you and trying to extricate information about your family." He dragged me to the bed and forced me to sit before gripping my face in his rough grasp. "I actually laughed at that request because I knew I'd have to do some real terrible things to get you to turn on your father."

My lips trembled at his threat-laced words. I knew what he meant. Their family enjoyed hacking off body parts one by one until someone confessed what they needed to know. The most ludicrous thing about it was that people lost consciousness or died before they had a chance to confess. At that point, you were a goner one way or another. Might as well take the words with you. I didn't pretend my family was that much better, but they were more creative, at least. And more effective.

A knock on the door dragged my attention away from Enzo. Before I could speak, he waved his hand.

"One of my men brought you some of the finest wine before bed, fit for a Silvani."

He opened the door and grabbed the tray with two wine glasses and a dark green bottle of wine. He set it on the dresser and filled a glass. The crimson liquid sloshed along the sides. I finished getting dressed, tugging on the least attractive shirt I owned. Enzo handed me one of the glasses as he sipped the other.

"Drink up, Gia," he said.

I licked my lips and looked him in the eyes, my chin raised in defiance. "I think I'd like to go home, Enzo," I said as I sniffed the wine and took a sip.

He laughed. "Oh no, that won't be possible. We're in this now. *Balls deep in it.*" His last words were sultry, as if they carried another meaning. Of course they did.

I downed the rest of my wine because I fucking needed it. "I'm just going to tell you this right now. We're *not* sleeping together, so you can stop trying to make hints. I hear them, and I'm not interested." My lip curled at him.

His face twisted. "Don't worry, I'm not trying to fuck you. I don't sleep with dogs. Your family is a stain and an embarrassment to all of us. Sylvester is a rich old family man who made some lucky choices. You guys aren't the crime bosses you think you are."

His words cut deep, offending my greatest ancestors. "Fuck you! Your family is *disgusting* and barbaric." I emphasized the word. They were disgusting. Blood had splattered and spilled across their family crest until it became unreadable.

"We don't have feds chasing our tail, unlike yours, so we barbarians must be doing something right."

"This was a big fucking mistake!" I yelled as he turned to walk away.

"For you, maybe." The door clicked shut behind him.

Chapter Five

Gia

I woke up to a bite of cold air that assaulted my skin, and it felt as if gritty grains of sand wiggled behind my eyelids. The dryness in my mouth rivaled that, like my tongue had been wiped with a cotton ball. My wrists burned against the rough rope that wound around them and attached me to a thick metal pole above my head. I was in some kind of basement, and that's about all I could glean from my surroundings. The walls were covered in plastic, as was the concrete beneath my feet. *Fuck, I know what that means.* I looked up at the ropes and tried to wiggle free, but it only burned and tugged at my skin the more I strained. The plastic barriers did nothing to deaden the shrill sound of my scream.

The upstairs door slammed, and footfalls thundered down wooden-plated steps. Enzo walked closer with a cold glaze to his eyes. He was the last person I wanted to see, but I'd hoped he would be the one to show up instead of his father or one of their goons.

"How'd I even get here?" I asked as I looked around the room. "Did you fucking drug me? I don't remember anything after you brought me a drink before bed."

"It was just a little family recipe." He raised my chin with his hand. "To be honest, we were fine with never getting the answer to this. Water under the bridge, right? But with such an opportunity, how could we pass up the chance to ask why your family was at the docks that day?"

"What? That was seven fucking years ago! You're lucky eighteen-year-old me didn't have the same firearm skills I have now." I rolled my eyes. "But you were ten years older than me, so there's no excuse for why you missed *me*."

Enzo's gaze fell for only a moment before he stared at me once more. His jacket slid back, and he grabbed the gun from his hip. He rubbed the gun's cold barrel against my cheek in a threatening gesture, not realizing how much having a firearm pointed my direction excited me. The rush of the risk of death. Someone else holding your life in the palm of their hand. That rush went straight to my pelvis and nestled there. But with Enzo's palm holding the gun, I was angry as much as I was excited.

Fuck him.

"Seven years ago, we lost the largest shipment we've ever lost, allowing your family to succeed us. I'm going to ask nicely again. Why was your family on the dock that day?"

"I don't know!" I shook my head.

"This is the part where I grab one of those many *excruciating* tools over there against the wall," he said as he gestured to the wall in front of me. The placement allowed his victims to watch as the weapon of destruction was chosen before their eyes, promising what sweet hell was to come. He rubbed his beard. "But I think showing your naked body to the man who killed your brother will hurt you much more than any hammer or loppers."

I recoiled at his words, remembering the day I became the eldest child. "Seriously, you're such a garbage human being. Such is this life." I mimicked my father's words, knowing I'd taken my revenge and killed one of his uncles about a year later. If he'd ever told his father what he saw, Silvio sure didn't act like it. *Why would he protect me, though?* "I'll take the pruners as my weapon of choice. Get it over with." My voice didn't quiver when I spoke. Fear was something that was earned, not given freely.

Enzo leaned into me, his mouth against my ear. "Why aren't you afraid? All Silvio would have to do is snap his fingers and I'd have to take care of you, Giovanna." His warm breath blanketed my neck and made goosebumps rise on my skin.

Of course I was scared, but there was a certain amount of responsibility I had as a crime lord's daughter. Part of that responsibility involved protecting our family's secrets.

Enzo

EVERY TOOL imaginable was laid out in front of me as I ran my hand along the table. Tools that had caused immeasurable suffering to our enemies, up to and including death. My fingers hovered above the hammer before running over the loppers. I gauged her reaction—or lack thereof—as I coiled my hand around the tool's cool plastic handle. With a smirk, I put the loppers down and picked up a sharp, curved knife. The blade reflected the light as I tapped it against the palm of my hand. My slow, methodical steps should have made her heart race, but if it did, she didn't show it. She knew better.

"Fuck you," she snarled.

I ran the blade along her clavicle as my gaze locked on her. The pent-up hatred I harbored for her family had spilled over onto her. She was a casualty of a war we didn't start.

The fabric spread as I cut down the length of her shirt, exposing her bra. She bit her lip and shook her head, which only fueled me further. That hurt her more than any weapon I could use on her. My fingers hooked the waistband of her pants and lowered the soft fabric as slowly as I could, teasing myself as much as I was torturing her. I hungered for the flesh beneath her panties. How could I not? As much as I hated her, her body was near perfection. Lucky for her—but not so much for me—I chose to leave the panties on. For now.

"Are you really going to pretend you don't know the answer?" I asked as I stepped behind her and pressed my crotch against her ass. I was certain she felt my excitement through my slacks as the curve of her ass fit perfectly against me. She had to know I would fuck her right there, that I would use her body like she ain't ever been used before. The only way to take her down a few notches would be to carve one into my bedpost.

She closed her eyes as I unclipped her bra, trembling as I wrapped my arm around her chest and held the fabric against her skin—her last chance to confess and stop me before I got my hands on her. A tear balanced on her eyelashes as she turned her head away, trying to hide it from me. But I saw. I felt a pang of . . . something . . . over making her shed even one tear. Fuck if I knew why.

"Fine." Her voice was so low that I almost didn't hear her over the hum of the furnace beside us. "The Riccis got hold of my father and told him to meet them at the docks for an investment opportunity," she said with a defeated breath.

I grazed the soft skin of her back as I clipped her bra again. A promise was a promise. "The Riccis? Are you sure?" I stepped in front of her, my head cocked.

"I'm positive."

"We were in business with them . . ." I paced a tight circle. "No . . . could they really have set us up to start a war?"

"If they did, they did it successfully."

I grabbed the knife and cut the fibrous ropes that held her wrists above her head. The rope frayed and spread, allowing her to pull her arms down. She rubbed her raw wrists, her lips pursed as she stared at me. Gia bent and pulled her pants up with a huff, and for a moment I worried she would go for one of the other weapons in the room. I hadn't thought that through.

I know what kind of woman Giovanna is. The kind who would stab me and paint her face with my blood.

Her torn shirt slipped down her shoulders, and she ripped it off and covered her chest with the remnants. "Garbage human," she said before bolting for the stairs.

I chased after her, but the moment she opened the door to the main floor, two of my men drew their pistols and aimed at her.

"Oh, fuck you too!" she yelled as she pushed them aside.

They cast confused looks at me before returning their attention to Gia, who refused to look back at any of us. The men gestured toward her with their barrels, expecting me to give the word to take the shot. I let the smirk fall from my face before lifting my hand and waving them off. They looked at each other and hesitated for a moment before dropping their pistols.

The sound of the slamming bedroom door ricocheted down the open hallway, vibrating the walls. I followed her path to the tall wooden door. Behind it, I heard her heavy breaths, as if she were finally letting herself feel her fear.

"Giovanna?" I taunted as my knuckle tapped on my side of the door.

"Leave me alone!" she yelled, an unusual shakiness in her words. She was always so confident, even when she wasn't.

"You didn't give me a chance to thank you for your information," I said with a strong hint of flirtation. I knew she didn't want it, but I enjoyed how much it pissed her off.

"Your appreciation is good enough, thanks."

Her annoyed response caused the corners of my lips to rise. The gap of light between the bottom of the door and the floor went black as she turned off the lights. I opened my hand and slapped the door. Message received.

Chapter Six

Gia

Iwoke up covered in sweat as I remembered what happened last night. The sun's rays split through the glass and painted an array of colors across the tan carpet. I put a hand to my head, fighting back a migraine as big as Enzo's ego. When I wiped the sleep from my eyes, I noticed a box on the table just inside the door. *The fuck?*

The carpet cushioned my feet as I crawled out of bed and headed toward the door. The light-blue box felt like leather in my hands as I brought it toward the bed. I lifted the top and it gave way with a squeak. My fingers grazed the silk of a deep red dress, the color of blood. *Of course.* I lifted the dress out of the box and held it up. It was beautiful, but I didn't want anything from him. The dress found its home back in its box, and I tossed it into the corner of the room, where it belonged.

The door creaked open, and Enzo walked into the bedroom. He crossed his arms over his chest at the sight of his discarded gift. "I take it you didn't like the dress?"

"It's fine, but I don't want anything from you. And I told you that." I sat on the bed and drew my legs toward my chest.

"You need something to wear that isn't jeans and pajamas if you're going to be around my family," he said as he lifted the box. He rifled through the contents and put it beside me on the bed.

"I don't plan on being here long enough to socialize with you people."

"Well, we requested the ransom yesterday, Giovanna, and it's been crickets so far. I hope you didn't get yourself in a position you can't flirt your way out of."

"If they don't pay, I can just go back home. No harm, no foul."

He tightened his lips. "You don't understand. There's both harm and foul. Silvio won't let you go back until they pay. We're invested in this now, and we aren't going to cause a rift between our families for nothing."

"So you're saying I was actually abducted?" I groaned as I dropped my face into my hands.

"Yes, but remember, this was your idea, not ours." He sat on the bed. "I want you to put the dress on."

I laughed humorlessly. "Fat chance."

"Do it, Giovanna." He tightened his lips and rubbed his hands along the front of his pants, smoothing the fabric. "I won't ask you again."

"Or what? What're you gonna do?"

He took a single deep breath. "Gia, I can make your time here easier, but you're making it very difficult for me to do so."

I offered him a blank stare. He was right. If his father took over as my guard, he would make my life hell until I wished for death. Enzo was the *kindest* of the three brothers, but that didn't say much for any of them. It was like ranking serial killers; they were all bad, just some worse than others.

Enzo was the oldest, and all three brothers had brooding good looks, but Enzo's eyes shone for their unique shade of blue that none of his brothers shared. Marco was the second oldest, a tall man who was known for lacking even a shred of sympathy in his entire body. He once shot a child because it was crying next to its dead mother. The youngest was Sammy, and he was a cookie cutter kid. He looked like a more handsome Silvio because he hadn't let himself grow into his father's wide stature.

I groaned, grabbed the box, and walked into the bathroom. My reflection stared back at me as I slipped off my shirt and let my pants fall to the floor. I held up the dress, rubbing my fingers along the soft material. It felt expensive. It probably was. When I pulled it on, it hugged my curves and shielded my cleavage a bit beneath the fine lace tracing the neckline. The dress was absolutely beautiful, I'd give him that, but it still wasn't what I wanted. I didn't want any of that.

I took a deep breath before I opened the door and stepped into the bedroom again. Even though I didn't care whether Enzo found me attractive or hideous—I didn't want him to find me anything at all—I felt bashful and kept my gaze on the ground.

"Wow," Enzo said as he drew my attention to him with a low groan. A smile crept across his face, and he didn't bother to hide the way his cock tented the front of his slacks.

"Don't try to be nice to me now," I said as I flashed him my bruised wrists.

He stood and came toward me, his full lips so close that I could almost taste his aftershave. Enzo wrapped his hand around the back of my neck and pulled me into him, letting his lips find me. I pulled away and looked up at him, his frame towering over me. Locks of his tousled black hair fell forward into his face. His eyes reached into mine and made me feel momentarily weak.

"Give me that mouth, Gia. I don't want to have to take it."

"Hard no," I whispered as I looked away from his crystal eyes. "You don't lay with dogs, remember?" I took another step away from him.

My body had responded to him and his words even though my mind was still very much disgusted by him. The way his lips pouted a bit as he looked at me, whether from hatred or attraction. Being able to see every inch of him through his black pants, every curve of his cock. He saw my weakening resolve. He was like a prowling animal, and I was injured prey trying to hide what ailed me.

I knew what the problem was. I'd starved my body of affection for so long that it ached for the wrong person—someone who was a part of the worst fucking family.

"Fine." He adjusted himself through his pants and flashed a tempting smile. "I thought we could have some fun, that's all."

Silence hovered in the air between us until he grew bored with waiting for me to change my mind. I had no intention of changing a damn thing.

If my pussy was on fire and he was the only one with water, I'd tell him to let me burn.

Chapter Seven

Enzo

We tried to be hospitable by inviting Gia to our kitchen table for breakfast, but she'd ignored our invitation so far. She snapped the olive branch I extended when I offered a Silvani a place at our table.

I popped a bagel out of the toaster and took a seat across from Silvio and beside my brother, Marco.

"She said the Riccis were involved?" Silvio raised a brow as he took a bite of his breakfast. "And you believe her?"

"I don't really see why she'd lie about that. I can't say that I'm terribly surprised, though, Pops. We took a risk by making a pact with them." I looked at Silvio's blank expression. As usual, he was impossible to read.

Gia's soft footfalls traveled toward us from the hallway. She leaned against the doorway, staring at us with all the hatred she deserved to carry. We went quiet, unwilling to have family conversations in front of an outsider. Especially not her.

I cleared my throat as she walked in and looked around the dining room. Her eyes hovered on the chandelier hanging between the large skylight windows.

Gia usually looked at me with ferocity in her every waking breath, and that morning was no different. She exhaled as she grabbed a banana and sat as far from me as possible at the table. My eyebrow raised as I watched her long fingers peel the yellow flesh, exposing the innards. Her perfect lips spread to take in the tip. I bit the inside of my lip. *Bitch gets me hard at my own damn table.* I expected her to blush when she noticed me staring, as if she'd realized it was a poor choice of fruit, but she just parted her full lips wider and took more of it in her mouth as she locked eyes with me.

"Gia, your parents still haven't responded to our request." Silvio tightened his lips, holding back his anger. He hated to be made a fool of, and Gia was making us all exactly that. "I don't think you're worth as much as you thought you were."

"Give it some time. They're probably pulling together the funds. It's not like we had that kind of money lying around the house."

"Yeah, yeah, we'll see," Silvio said as he wiped his mouth and put the napkin on the table with a slam of his fist. "You know, Miss Silvani, we can give you more freedom here, but you have to earn it."

I knew what Silvio meant. He would happily take her to bed to give her *all* the freedom she wanted. He'd make her his whore. He'd ruin her, but she'd destroy him in return. The thought of him fucking her made my lips curl. If anyone was going to fuck her, it would be me.

Gia

THE SUN WARMED my back as we walked along one of the paved paths around the mansion. Enzo looked at me sideways every so often, the sun reflecting in his eyes.

"I'm glad I was *allowed* to go for a walk," I said with an annoyed snap of the word.

"It's not only to keep you from leaving, Gia. It's not safe out here alone. You know as well as I do that silence is only trouble that hasn't happened yet." He flashed his eyes at me once more. "You'd be an easy target out here."

Enzo's muscles flexed as he put his hand on top of his gun. My wandering eyes followed his movements, lingering on the tattoos blanketing his arm. Black ink covered the curves of his muscles—a mobster in a fedora with smoke rising from his cigarette and surrounding him; a half-naked woman straddling an intricate, tilted cross. The woman must have been a recent addition. The last time I'd seen that tattoo, it only depicted the cross with beads that dangled in the shape of a noose. I recognized the firearms with smoking barrels dotting other areas of his arms—an M16 and a revolver, among others. A hint of more ink on his back peeked from beneath his ribbed sleeveless shirt. *Oh god, stop looking at him.* I tried to remind myself who this man was and what family he was from.

I turned my gaze away when he noticed me staring. A grin crawled across his face, and his eyebrow raised.

Oh, fuck you.

"Where are we going?" I asked.

"The indoor pool," he said as he gestured toward a large building detached from the main house.

"I don't really—"

"Well, you don't really have much of a choice." He smiled as he wrapped his arm around my back and dragged me into him. I cringed at his touch.

We walked through a metal door once Enzo unlocked it, and the smell of chlorine and sweat assaulted my nose the moment we stepped foot inside. The building was empty and pin-drop quiet except for the gurgle of the pool filter. My jaw dropped as I looked around. Rock landscaping surrounded the pool and color changing lights dotted the bottom, causing a rippling effect in the water. Steam rose off the hot tub. Huge skylight windows looked down on the pool while a wall of windows overlooked the courtyard, letting sunshine into the room at every corner. The wooden ceilings gave the building a rustic vibe, and pendant lights shined above the pool.

I lifted my jaw from the floor. "It's clear where your family spends your money. My god."

"I thought we could take a swim?" He grinned at me. If he hadn't been Enzo from the infamous Viglione family, it would have seemed like a genuine gesture. For the Vigliones, there was no such thing. They never did anything they wouldn't see a return on, and I knew what Enzo wanted.

Not going to happen.

"I don't have a bathing suit," I said as I kneeled to touch the warm water in the heated pool. The temperature was perfect, like everything else in that fucking building.

"You're wearing a bra and underwear, aren't you?" He pulled off his undershirt before I could reply, exposing his muscular stomach and chest. With a body like that, I could *almost* look past what an asshole he was. His intense blue eyes remained locked on mine as he unfastened his belt. It was slow and methodical and meant to leave me weak with desire.

It'll take more than that.

His black pants slipped past his thighs and he stepped out of them, folding them before placing them on a table. I bit my cheeks to remind my jaw to stay where the fuck it was as my gaze hovered at his boxer briefs. The outline of his cock was perfectly drawn, nearly popping from the bottom of his underwear.

Why is it suddenly so hot in here?

"Your turn," he said as he rubbed his beard.

I looked down at my shorts and t-shirt and decided they were worth sacrificing. There wasn't a chance in hell he would get me down to my bra and panties. I slipped into the hot tub, and steam rose and embraced my face as it swirled around me. My clothes clung to my body, and the warmth and security of it enveloped me. It made me miss home.

Enzo followed me into the hot tub, and a quiet groan escaped my throat as he slid in. *Great.* The water rose slightly as he submerged himself and draped his arm over the side of the tub. I eyed the head and coiling body of a viper wrapped around the inside of his arm, burying its fangs in his flesh. He brushed a hand through his hair, which left it wet and slicked back. Drops of water dribbled down his forehead, across his nose, and onto his lip. He blew them away and dropped his head back.

Focus.

"So, Giovanna . . . are you going to tell me why you're really here?"

"I told you why I'm here," I said flatly, brushing my hair back with a wet hand. *Mostly.*

"I want to hear it from those beautiful lips of yours." He lifted his head and flashed me a flirty grin that twisted my stomach as much as it shocked me awake between my legs. I had to remind my body to stop reacting to such a piece of shit.

I shook my head, unwilling to play his games. When I saw him staring at the way my clothes clung to my breasts, I shielded them behind crossed arms. "I'm not telling you shit, Enzo." I stood, sending water rushing over the side of the tub as I climbed out. I sat in a chair by the pool and rested my cheek on my fist. Water dripped from my clothes and gathered in puddles around me.

"I feel like you've forgotten what happened when we were younger." Enzo smirked, and his body flexed as he lifted himself over the edge of the hot tub, his skin red from the heat of the water.

"Oh, please." I waved him away with my hand, dismissing his version of the "memory."

He stood and left a trail of water in his path as he walked toward me. His hands rubbed down my arms and landed on the metal chair, gripping with a harshness that didn't surprise me, even if I hadn't expected it. He leaned close to my ear, and his warm breath rushed over my neck.

"I fucked the daughter of Sylvester Silvani."

His words sent shivers up my spine. Mostly from annoyance, but a sliver of it was from the gravelly tone of his voice. My fingers wrapped around the arm of the chair and squeezed. I had lain with the enemy once, many years ago, when I had just turned eighteen. Before the day at the docks. I said that most of the men I slept with ended up dead. Well, he was one who didn't, unfortunately. Here he was, alive and fucking well in front of me. He was as good as dead to me, though.

"Do you remember it yet?" he asked, his tone more insistent this time.

"Hardly," I said. "Guess it wasn't that memorable."

Of course I remembered. We were at a house party for the father of a mutual ally. Out of respect for him and his death at the hands of the FBI—the worst kind of death—everyone was inclined to leave their rivalries at the door. Apparently, I also left my panties at the door. I was young, horny, and stupid. Enzo had just happened to walk by the balcony overlooking the city, and he gave me the same sensual "fuck me" look he tried to use in the mansion. It had worked back then, but now? He might as well save his energy. There wasn't a chance in hell he would get me bent over the railing with my dress hiked up my waist again. He shook up my family when he killed my brother.

I'd rather die.

"Interesting," he said as he knelt in front of me.

His hand raced up my thigh. The moment I opened my mouth to tell him to fuck off, he moved my shorts aside. I tried to push him away with my knee, but not before he managed to rub two fingers between my legs. He bit his lip as he glanced up at me, and for a single moment, I imagined his face between my thighs.

"For someone who doesn't remember anything, you sure are wet."

He withdrew his hand, and a trail of my unintentional wetness clung to his finger as he pulled away from me. My body had no idea who she was fucking with. My face flushed and I slammed my thighs together. Enzo sneered as he wiped his hand off on my leg.

"My body *may* like you, but my mind fucking hates you," I snarled.

"It ain't your mind I wanna sink into, Gia," he growled.

Chapter Eight

Enzo

Gia's stunning body rode me. Her thighs surrounded mine and squeezed. My hands raced along her sides as her head dropped back in pleasure, and for this moment, we never had a rivalry between us. There was nothing between us.

Her breasts were just as I remembered. Full and heavy, tanned skin visible in the valley between them. She leaned down and pressed her lips to mine as she moved against me. I was going to come, and I bucked my hips as I gripped hers. My muscles tightened and I was about to—

The alarm clock blared beside my head, waking me at the worst possible moment—just as I was about to unload inside her pussy. *That fucking girl.* I rubbed the painfully hard erection in my shorts and dropped my head back with a sigh. Seeing between her legs had stirred up a lot of memories. I still remembered how she felt and how I made her feel back then, during the moment she forgot we were enemies.

To be clear, Gia was never *my* enemy. Our parents' enemies became ours, just as their parents' enemies became theirs. It went on and on until we couldn't remember why we hated each other in the first place. I was *her* enemy, though, and I knew why she hated me. She would always despise me for killing her brother that night at the docks. I rearranged their family.

Her brother and I were in a standoff, and only one of us could walk out of there. I chose me. That exact moment happened to her a year later, between my uncle and her. She hesitated for a moment, trying to figure out if murder was really necessary. His trigger finger moved just a hair, but enough to make her react. The deafening gunshot echoed through the deserted subway station. She had no remorse as she holstered the smoking gun and walked away.

I was supposed to choose my family over her, but I didn't. When facing Silvio, I told him I didn't see who'd done it. Why? Beats me.

I slipped out of bed and began to get dressed. My soft dress pants rubbed against my skin as I pulled them on. I slid hangers across the bar as I tried to pick out a crisp dress shirt, landing on one in a shade of deep purple, one of my favorites. I draped my jacket over my shoulder and left my room. When I stepped foot into the main house, I walked into Silvio.

"Enzo," he said, his breath heavy, as if he'd jogged from his side of the damn house.

"Last I checked," I quipped.

He took a deep breath, trying to steady his chest. "The Silvanis didn't pay. Complete silence. Not even a fucking no."

I scoffed. "Why do I think we got stuck with the fucking broad?"

"If they don't pay up, I'll take my payment in her pussy and then some."

Silvio's words rubbed me all the wrong ways. Fuck if I knew why, but I wanted him to forget the idea of sleeping with Gia. No one else was getting into her.

Gia

THE CEILING FAN circled above my head, and I stared at it in a near trance. The door slammed and brought my attention back to the four tan walls surrounding me. I sat up and gasped at the sight of Silvio in my room. This vile man was the last person I wanted to see.

As he walked over and sat beside me, the buttons of his jacket strained against his gut, and each forceful exhale made him sound as if he were congested. His large, tan hand reached for my thigh, his fingers making imprints on my skin as he grasped me roughly. I tried to scoot away from him, but he grabbed my waist and held me in place.

"Your parents still haven't paid," he said as his hand left my thigh to brush my hair away from my face. He groaned as his fingers laced around the back of my neck. I stared straight ahead, my lower lip trembling as his hand traced my thigh again. They wouldn't pay, meaning I'd trapped myself within a den of starving lions.

The bedroom door opened again, and my stomach dropped. I knew their M.O. when it came to sexual assault. It became a family affair. I'd heard of the things they'd done, and I wanted nothing to do with it.

"What are you doing?" Enzo's voice broke the silent tension between me and his father.

I kept calm and refused to show fear to either of them. They couldn't break me, not if I didn't allow it.

"I'm just having a little fun with her." Silvio raised his hands defensively.

Enzo crossed the room, and Silvio stood to square off with him. Even though he was shorter than Enzo, his stature wasn't where his power came from. Enzo's eyes narrowed as he stared down his father. It was clear he didn't want to argue with Silvio in front of me, and their expressions allowed them to communicate without words.

"You're making a mistake by coming at me like this, son. This ain't over," he said as he left the room.

Enzo stared at him as he left, his face twisted as if he knew he'd be punished for it later.

A part of me expected Enzo to comfort me or apologize, but he didn't and he wouldn't. He lifted his jacket from his shoulder and placed it on the table beside the bed.

He sat and stared at me. "If you didn't wear such skimpy clothes—"

"They are fucking shorts, Enzo. Are you kidding me?" I snapped.

"Eh, he wouldn't have done anything anyway. You're a Silvani," he said with an annoyed snap as he waved his hand at me.

"You know, I'm getting real sick and tired of you talking shit about my family. You aren't any different from us, and in many ways, you're worse. If you want my honest opinion, you disgust me," I told him firmly, making my feelings very clear.

"That may be, but ya still wanna fuck me. So what does

that say about you?" He furrowed his brow at me, and his lips pouted slightly.

Goddamn it, that look.

Enzo grasped the back of my neck in the same way his father had. I shivered at his touch and shook my head. He pulled me into him and kissed me, his full lips spreading on mine. I put my hands up to his chest and tried to push him back, but his body was immovable as his kisses grew hungrier.

The touch of his father scared me—not that I would admit it—but Enzo's forceful touch didn't. It didn't rattle me to my core, not that I would admit that, either.

"No." I took a deep breath as I pulled away from him.

He pushed me down on the bed and put his arms on either side of my head, his muscles flexing. A low groan left his mouth as he pressed his hips against mine, his cock rubbing me through my shorts. His revolver in its holster swirled my thoughts. He looked down at me with disgustingly intoxicating eyes, the rich blue color half hidden behind his eyelids as he stared at me. My body reacted to him against my will, defying me as my top teeth bit into my lower lip.

"It's definitely a no?" His voice was harsh yet seductive as the soft fabric of his dress pants brushed against my inner thighs. He grinded his hips, rubbing his hard dick against me. It sent unwelcome tingles from my pelvis into my stomach.

"No," I said. "I mean yes, yes it's a no." I choked over my words. "No," I said more firmly that time, trying to convince myself as much as I needed to convince him. He rubbed a hand down my cheek, and it hovered around my throat. I swallowed hard.

"Alright, suit yourself," he said as he sat up and stood.

His cock pressed against the inside of his pants, and I saw the length of him again.

Goddamn it.

He rubbed a hand through his beard. "You know, I could fuck ya a lot better than when we were younger."

"We won't be finding out," I said.

He smirked. "We'll see about that."

Chapter Nine

Gia

Who the fuck does he think he is? I stared at the words on a folded piece of paper I found on my bed after I got out of the shower.

Meet me on the balcony tonight at seven. Wear the dress.

I crumpled the paper into a tight ball and looked at the big gold hands working their way around the face of the clock. 5:30 *p.m.* The dress glared at me from the box on the bed. *Not a fucking chance.*

I picked up the dress and spread it in front of me. *I'll just look.* A frustrated groan left my lips as I did a circle with it against me, allowing the long skirt to flow around me. *God, this is beautiful.*

To put on this dress meant I agreed to his invitation, and that wasn't what I wanted . . . right? The fabric answered my question as I slid it over my body. The silky material clung to me, exciting my skin. The slit on the side rode up my leg and stopped at my thigh. My reflection stared back at me in the bathroom mirror. Without any tools to style my hair, it fell in messy waves. I grabbed the lipstick from the little clutch on the counter, opened the cap, and brushed the deep red onto my pouty lips.

When I opened the bedroom door and peered into the hallway, I tripped over a pair of black heels. *Now it's my turn to play with him.* I smiled as I brushed my hands along my hips.

Enzo

THE HANDS on the gold watch on my wrist ticked past seven. I brushed my hand through my hair to calm my frayed nerves. The tapping sound of heels behind me made my heart skip a beat, but I didn't dare turn around. I waited and rested my head against my hand as Gia appeared in front of me.

Oh god, she looks fucking incredible. Those lips, the swells of her breasts ready to burst from the fabric, and those goddamn hips . . .

"Hey," I said, a smug look on my face. The red of her dress matched my dress shirt. "What made you come?"

"I wanted a reason to wear something other than pajamas, that's all," she said as she sat in the chair across from me. Her face was unreadable, and I maintained my poker face as my eyes scanned her body.

One of my men came onto the balcony, staring at Gia like a hungry dog.

"What do ya want to drink?" the man asked me.

"Bring me a bottle of bourbon, and for her? A red wine."

"I can order for myself, thank you." She looked up at the man beside us. "Just the bourbon is fine."

The corners of my lips twitched upward as I nodded toward him. "Bourbon it is, I guess."

After he returned and poured our drinks, I played with the rim of the glass with my index finger as Gia swished the dark liquid.

"Why aren't you drinking?" She stopped mid-sip. "Oh god, you aren't trying to drug me again, are you?" She placed her glass on the table and pushed it toward the center.

I leaned over, grabbed her glass, and downed it. "No, I wasn't drugging you." As I pushed my drink toward her, the bottom of my full glass scraped against the table.

"With my luck, you drugged this one, knowing I would ask you about that one." She pointed toward the empty glass. Her eyes narrowed. "I don't trust you."

"What would I get from drugging you, Gia? Come on."

"I know what you'd take if I was drugged." Gia pushed the glass back toward me.

"I don't need to drug you to take that." I gestured toward her lap and raised my eyebrow. "Besides, I'd want you awake to *feel every inch of me.*" My head filled with thoughts of her doing just that.

She blew hair from her forehead before standing and walking to the balcony's railing, looking across the courtyard as she leaned over it. She was teasing me, and she knew it. Her hips wiggled slightly as she shifted her weight from one leg to the other. Seeing her in that familiar position made me painfully hard and sent an aching throb through my cock. My mind raced with thoughts of taking her. I dropped my head back and sighed.

She wants to play? I'll play. I walked over to her, grabbing her hips firmly and allowing my breath to roll over her neck as she looked back at me. Her eyelashes fluttered as she stared at me.

"I don't want you to fuck me," she said.

"I don't need to fuck you."

I grabbed her, turned her to face me, and lifted her. She squealed as she looked down at me, her legs wrapping around my hips. Her skirt slid up her thighs as I laid her on the patio table, knocking off the bottle of bourbon and the glasses. The glass crashed to the concrete floor, shattering into pieces. The smell of liquor hung in the air. Our eyes locked as I pushed the dress up her thighs so slowly that goosebumps rose on her skin. My gaze dropped to the black panties between her legs hiding what I craved. What I needed. I snatched her panties aside, exposing her incredible pussy. The same one that squeezed the come from my cock in my dreams.

I began to devour her. Her body was tense beneath my touch, as if she wanted me to stop. I couldn't stop. A soft moan left her parted lips as her chest rose, arching her back. She was so wet that it dripped from her, and I lapped it up. She tasted sweet, how I imagined she would taste if I ever had the chance to lay her in front of me. Her thighs trembled as her hands gripped the edges of the table.

"I'm going to c—" she began to whisper, her legs shaking.

I stopped all movement of my mouth, and she looked down at me with a shocked expression and her lips parted.

"What the fuck?"

"I didn't say you could come yet," I growled as I traced around her clit with my finger, refusing to put any pressure directly on it.

"What the fuck do you mean?" She rose onto her elbows and went to close her legs, but I held them open.

"I also didn't say it's time to stop." My arms flexed as I spread her legs again.

She looked bewildered, and I was fine with that. I wanted her to want that orgasm so badly it made her sick. Once she breathed evenly again, I dove into her, letting my tongue work her all over again. Every lick brought her closer and closer. Her muscles began to tense again, and the familiar quivering of her thighs vibrated against my shoulders. She tried not to tell me when she was going to come, but I could feel the moment she began teetering on the edge of her orgasm.

So I stopped.

"No, no, no, come on!" She dropped her head back, and her thighs tried to clamp shut, to cause friction to push her over the edge I dangled her from.

"Ah, ah," I scolded as I kept her thighs spread.

"No, fuck you, Enzo," she said as she tried to scoot away from me.

I grabbed her hips and held her in front of me. She wasn't going anywhere.

When her pleasure had been replaced by her anger, I gave her what she wanted again. My tongue worked her in slow, even strokes, the pleasure filling her body with every flick. I caught her dripping wetness with my tongue and slid up, curling my tongue at her clit. Her moans grew, breaking the silence of the night air once more. Each time I brought her toward the edge and stopped her descent, she was easier and easier to bring to that point again.

She grabbed my hair and tugged as if she could keep me from pulling away with just her measly grasp. Her body begged for release before her mouth could, and she let out a frustrated scream as I pulled away from her and wiped my mouth. Gia covered her face with her hands and sighed. She was pissed she'd let me go down on her. And angrier I couldn't at least make her come.

"You're a fucking piece of shit," she hissed as she pulled her skirt down. "Really?"

"I didn't say you could come yet." I grinned at her. "And it won't be tonight." I reached over, brushed her hair back, and kissed her. With a light touch, I slid my hand between her legs again and she shuddered against me.

"Fuck you!" she yelled as she stood and kneed me in the groin.

My cheeks puffed and my lips tightened as I tried to keep my composure. She was lucky I wouldn't hurt her. Not for just being Gia, that is. Wasn't that what attracted me to her, after all?

Chapter Ten

Gia

My thoughts raced as I passed framed family pictures in the hallway on my way toward my room. I cursed at every image I passed with Enzo's stoic posture in it, never willing to smile. *Fucking bastard.* I slammed the door to the bedroom and dropped the heels I'd been carrying. My legs were still shaky as the denial radiated through my body. Hatred for him coursed through my blood—except when it rushed to the area between my thighs, apparently. I made the mistake of letting myself be vulnerable *one time*, and that was how he handled my vulnerability? I refused to allow that to happen again.

I flopped onto the bed with a sigh as visions of the evening raced through my mind. Which made me that much angrier. *Fuck you, Enzo.* The ache between my legs intensified the longer I went unsatiated. The desire urged my hands to walk along the inside of my thighs, every graze of my fingertips feeling like electricity. I felt the warmth of wet excitement between my legs as I spread them. The thought of his perfect fucking mouth on—

A knock on the door startled me just as I began to play between my legs. I covered myself with my dress and sat up when the door opened. Enzo stood in the doorway, the light from the hallway illuminating his muscular frame.

"I thought I told you that you weren't going to get off tonight," he said.

How did he know? I put my hands up to my cheeks, flushed with frustration, trying to not look like I got caught with my hand in the proverbial cookie jar. I looked around the room and spotted a tiny camera in the corner, nearly flush with the ceiling. A piece of black tape blocked the red indicator. I gasped, dropping my hands from my face. The flushing of my cheeks could have easily been caused by anger now. And it was.

"You're spying on me? Are you kidding me?"

"That ol' thing? No, I just knew what you would come in here and do. I'm not stupid, Gia." The low, seductive way he spoke made me sick. I'd have thrown up on his fancy fucking shoes if I could have.

"You don't own me, Enzo. Even though I'm stuck here, you don't have the control over me you think you do."

His eyes squinted at me as he stepped closer. He pulled out his phone and hit a button as he looked up at the camera. "Do you really want to challenge me?" He hovered over me. My lip trembled. "Lorenzo has been begging me to let him get at you, and if I see you touch yourself, I will grant him his wish. Please don't make me do that. He wouldn't be very nice to you." Enzo roughly brushed his hand through my hair and lifted my chin. "I will choose when you come, if I let you come at all." He smirked in a grin that made my panties melt and my blood pressure rise.

Enzo turned to leave and just as he reached the door, he turned back toward me. "Keep your hands where I can see them, babygirl."

The door slammed and silence washed over me again. I stared at the camera, anger rising in my gut. "Fuck you!" I yelled toward it.

I grabbed some clothes and went into the bathroom to change. The dress hung heavy with the new secrets it held, and I let it fall to the floor. I slipped on a long t-shirt and a pair of shorts, the most unattractive outfit I could come up with. I looked at myself in the mirror and gasped as I wiped the smudged makeup off my cheeks.

I look like a mess. Why did I agree to this? I'm in a den with a goddamn wolf.

When I walked back into the bedroom, I flipped my middle finger toward the camera, crawled into bed, and wrapped the covers around me. The soft sheets encased me, soothing my angry skin and calming my nerves. Before long, the restlessness overcame me and I threw myself onto my back, kicking at the heaviness of the blankets around my feet.

"I hope you can hear me, Enzo. Threatening me with rape isn't going to get you into my pants, you fucking prick," I said as I turned away from the camera again. "*And* you wouldn't even do the job yourself? You'd send someone else to do the dirty work?" I pulled the blanket over my head. "Pussy!" I nearly yelled the insult as I hurled it at the camera.

S‍leep escaped me as the buzzing alarm clock broke the silence like a cloud of bees swarming around the nightstand. I didn't remember falling asleep, but I sure as shit remembered everything that happened before I did. The moment I thought about Enzo, my stomach tightened with a confusing swirl of hatred and curiosity. I groaned as I lay on my back and stared at the ceiling. The fan moved at a slow pace, swirling the air.

I threw off the blanket and stood. My foot knocked into my bag, and I squatted to rummage through it. I felt around the front pocket until I held the comfort of the little black button-sized audio recorder in my hand. *I thought for sure he'd have found this when he searched my shit. Maybe this won't all be for nothing after all.* I kept my body strategically placed between my bag and the camera's line of sight as I put the recorder back into my bag and crawled into bed again. I wasn't ready to get up and face a single Viglione today. Instead, I covered my body with the down blanket to let myself be lulled to sleep by the comfort of knowing I wouldn't be the only one recorded. *He's forgotten who he's dealing with. Who my family is. He may have won this battle, but I'll win the war.*

Chapter Eleven

Enzo

"**A**re you losing it?" I said to Silvio. My voice ricocheted off the barren walls in the library. This room was merely used for meetings, with empty bookshelves rising from the ground to the tall ceilings.

Silvio took an intimidating step toward me. "Don't talk to me like that, Enzo."

"You did a hit in broad daylight! Are you trying to get us all caught? I ain't going down for you being fucking reckless." I threw my hands up and pushed the wheeled chair away from me. Silvio's hits had become more brazen, and that wasn't how we operated. It wasn't how we kept the feds out of our business. Silvio was trying to put a neon sign above our goddamn heads.

"This particular target would have been impossible to get in a situation that you would consider acceptable, so drop it." Silvio raised his hand dismissively. His fat cheeks puffed out and hid the corners of his mouth.

"Two hundred thousand is enough to risk all of—" My lips pursed. "Just forget it. You're losing it, old man."

"You think you can run this family better than me? Is that what you think?"

Silvio grabbed the collar of my shirt and pulled me into him. His hot breath brushed along my chest. I knew better than to talk back further at this point, so I kept my mouth shut. Silvio had killed one of his own brothers for speaking out against the family. Being his flesh and blood meant nothing to him.

He released my shirt and drew a long exhale. "Watch yourself, Enzo."

I stared at him, my eyes squinting in frustration. I slammed my fist down on a small circular table beside us and sent papers scattering to the floor. There were no words I could say that wouldn't piss him off, so I left him yelling obscenities as I walked away and slammed the door behind me. His words followed me until the door sealed behind me, dropping a curtain of silence in the hallway.

My steps echoed down the big open hall as I stormed toward the wooden double doors at the other end. Frustration poured out of me with every heavy footfall, and sweat beaded on my forehead as anger rose into my chest. My heartbeat pounded in my ears.

What a goddamn fool! There was only one thing I could think of when I was this angry, and it was sinking my cock into the mouth of some broad and fucking her face until I was too tired to be mad.

Once I reached the door, I didn't even knock. I just pushed it open. I used more force than I intended, and the doorknob crashed into the wall, cracking a hole in the drywall. My entrance startled Gia, as if I were a monster. *Which I am.*

"What the fuck!" she yelled as she held her towel closer to her body. She stopped changing in the main room once she knew about the camera, preventing me from enjoying my favorite show every night. Rookie mistake on my part.

With the heat of anger coursing through my veins, I felt the intense desire to take her. Not just take her, but to break her. She would be no easy woman to get beneath me. It would be a fight, and I got hard at the thought of her crying as she told me to stop. Her words from last night replayed in my head, taunting me. She had some nerve to think I wouldn't take what I wanted. I had only kept her pussy largely untouched out of respect for her as a guest in my home, but if she wanted to play games and poke the bear, I'd show her what it was like to get ripped to shreds.

My eyes scanned her body. The towel did nothing to hide her sensual curves. My hungry glare didn't scare her, which annoyed the fuck out of me. How dare she forget who I was. I let her get away with her smart-ass mouth and even kneeing me in the goddamn nuts, but I was done letting her be the puppet master when she had no control here.

She caught my gaze and clutched the towel closer. "What are you doing here, Enzo?"

Like a predator closing the distance between myself and my prey, I walked toward her and answered her question with a rough kiss. She pushed me away with one hand while the other held her towel in a sure grasp. Her wet hair felt like silk in my hand as I fisted it at the nape of her neck.

"Don't!" she said with a firm snap of the word. In the face of predation, women like Gia puffed themselves up to make themselves look bigger. She didn't become a fearful little girl in my hands. She became a lioness.

"Here's the thing, babygirl. I need to have you." I looked

down at her, watching her lip quiver. That was the only sign that showed me she was the least bit scared. Or excited. Who fucking knew with her. "Remember what you said last night?"

"Which part?"

"You called me a pussy because I wouldn't take you myself," I growled against her neck. "Do I really need to prove just how far I'm willing to go to get what I want?" I bit into my lower lip. My cock throbbed against the zipper of my pants.

Her lip twitched, and I knew Gia enough to know that she had some smart-ass response she was trying to hold back. Her unwillingness to submit to me only turned me on more. I'd never had a bitch that brave in front of me, and I fucking *needed* to have her beneath me. I wanted to see how brave she'd be when I made her take every inch of me, taking all her confidence and bravado and ripping it away from the inside.

My hand reached for her thigh, squeezing her soft flesh before driving my hand under her towel. She gasped as my prying fingers rubbed between her legs. Her attempts to push me away grew weaker until her hand merely rested on my shoulder.

"Please," she whispered as she looked up at me, her dark eyes encased in long black lashes. I couldn't tell if she was pleading for more or for me to stop. The wetness coating my fingers made me lean toward her wanting more.

Well, shit.

"What do you want, Giovanna?" Her name fell from my lips so effortlessly.

Her thighs trembled at the sound of my voice. Desire for her hid beneath my words, and she knew it. I sank my fingers inside her, drawing them back out to rub her clit. When she glared at me, I palmed her.

"I want . . ." Her chest rose and fell as if her heart was about to leap from her chest. "I want you . . . to go fuck yourself." Her voice was woven with pleasure until the last four words. She smirked as she took a step back from me, tightened her towel, and crossed her arms over her chest.

I brought my fingers up to my mouth and licked them, tasting her. Her scent and sweetness brought me right back to the balcony, with her laid out in front of me. Everything about her was delicious and she fucking knew it.

Everything except her goddamn attitude and bloodlines.

"I don't need to fuck myself when I got you," I snarled.

I grabbed her and pushed her down on the bed. I ripped the towel open, exposing her perfect body. Tits that would make anyone weak in the damn knees, enemy or not. Her arms flailed and pushed against me as I worked my zipper down and lowered the front of my boxers, letting my cock drop between her legs. The momentary flash of fear on her face almost made me bust right then, ready to coat her pretty little pussy if I couldn't sink inside it.

"Fuck right off, Enzo," she said through clenched teeth.

She wouldn't let them fall, but I saw the tears welling and glossing her eyes. She'd probably let me take her before she'd let me see her cry like that. Instead, she drew her arm back and punched me in the jaw, her ring grazing my cheek. I growled and pinned her wrists above her head. The heat between her legs radiated toward me as I leaned over her. My cock was so close to what I wanted that my dick grew wet as it lay against her. My gaze shot to the camera in the corner, and I slammed my fist on the bed beside her head. She screamed, as if she thought I would hit her.

Of the many things I would do to her, hitting her wasn't one of them.

"Fuck," I said, backing away from her.

She stared at me as I pulled up my boxers, my throbbing cock veiled but still clearly visible. The way she stared at me made me raise my eyebrow at her. She didn't look scared or angry. She somehow looked disappointed, as if she wanted it as much as I did.

Not like this, I tried to remind myself. I brushed my hand through my hair and released a heavy breath.

With a huff, she stood and smacked me. My cheek stung and I reached my hand up to it—the same place where her ring had cut me. I dabbed at the blood, taking a deep breath to remind myself to remain in control. She loved to fuck with me. When I made her face the prize I'd won, she'd wish she hadn't played around. It would be her, and it wouldn't be sweet and loving. I'd destroy her and love every goddamn moment of it.

How the fuck do I explain this? There was no explaining how Gia got a hit on me while remaining unscathed. I'd be weak in my family's eyes. My lip curled as I grabbed her hair and jerked her toward me. "I'm really trying not to hurt you, Gia."

"Clearly," she said as she rubbed her hand along the front of my boxers, becoming a player in my game.

The simple feel of her touch lit my nerves on fire. My thoughts whirled with ill intentions all over again. I shook my head as I released her hair.

She narrowed her eyes. "What do you call what you just tried to do?"

"What you want," I snarled.

"You really are a goddamn pussy," she quipped with a

humorless laugh before grabbing her towel and wrapping it around her once more.

My eyes closed and I took a deep breath to cleanse my thoughts. It worked in the sense that I didn't bend her little ass over and fuck her then and there. I opened my eyes, tilting my head in a way that made her bite her lip when she looked at me. I pressed her back against the wall and pinned her. My hand wrapped around her throat and lifted her just enough to make her *finally* show the fear I wanted to see on her face. I could hurt her, kill her even, if I chose to. She wasn't the bad bitch she portrayed outside of this house.

Realization washed over me. How wet she was, the words she used to nip me in the hopes I'd bite her back, and how she sucked on her lower lip.

"You fucking want it, don't you?" I growled as I pressed my body against hers, my painfully hard cock still pressed against her stomach through my boxers. "Well, fuck, that changes everything." A smile meant for the devil crossed my lips.

She looked at me with a pout as I lowered her until her feet landed on the ground.

"I won't be fucking you, Giovanna. Not your pussy, at least. I'll be fucking your mind." I tapped her forehead.

"What the fuck does that even mean?"

I grabbed her hand and placed it on my boxers, directly over my cock. "I will make you want this so fucking bad you'll be dreaming of me. You'll beg me to make you come."

Her hand dropped back to her side and mine wandered between her legs. She melted against the wall as I rubbed her until her breaths grew ragged. I slammed my fingers into her, drove them harder and faster inside her until moans escaped her lips no matter how much she tried to keep them sealed away. Her abdomen clenched as she drove her hips into me. As her hands gripped the towel, I stopped.

I fucking stopped.

Like a puppy desperate for my attention, she leaned into me, letting her lips find mine, as if that would make me let her come. It only fueled my desire to play with her head. I pulled my hand away from her, and her hips followed my movement. She grabbed my hand, looking up at me with big eyes, and I nearly pushed her to her knees so I could see them beneath my cock. She brought my fingers to her full lips, letting her tongue swirl around them.

Fucking touché.

Even that wasn't enough to make me give in to her. I zipped up my pants, buttoning them with a smirk on my face.

"You're a piece of shit, Enzo."

"Yeah, so you've told me."

Chapter Twelve

Gia

The door creaked open and I clenched my eyes shut, knowing it was Enzo. I was still pissed at him. He was as repulsive as he was hot, which was fucking annoying. My head hated him, but everything else wanted him on or inside it.

"Fuck off, Enzo!" I yelled without turning over, refusing to give him the satisfaction of my attention.

He didn't respond, but heavy footsteps approached from behind. I lifted myself onto my elbow to pivot my body toward him, but a large hand wrapped around my mouth before I could change positions. With very little effort, he dragged me out of bed and I stumbled to my feet as his arm wrapped around me, his dick pressing against me.

"Finally," the voice whispered.

Panic strummed through me as I realized the voice did *not* belong to Enzo. I balled my hand into a fist and slammed it backward, hitting the man in the nuts. The front of his body fell into me as he groaned against the pain. I slipped out of his grasp and tried to run toward the door, but he grabbed my hair, reeling me toward him and slamming me onto my back. My hands reached for the hair in his grasp, trying to stop the searing pain in my scalp. As he dragged me to my knees, I finally realized who it was. Lorenzo. My heart sank so deep into my gut I thought it would disappear.

I knew what he wanted, what they always wanted. Raping the daughter of Sylvester Silvani was a challenge men like him had met on more than one occasion. Assaulting me was almost more delicious to them than killing me. If they merely shot me, I couldn't walk around with the memory of them inside me. When nervous fear ran up my thighs at a man's touch, they'd get off on knowing they'd planted that seed of panic.

The worst was when my father tried to claim money for a debt from another family. Then they claimed me. All three brothers. They took turns with me in the back room of a club. Even then, I refused to cry. I couldn't allow them to see my tears, even as their hands pressed my face into the rough, curtain-lined walls as I tried to figure out what I'd done to deserve it. I didn't create their debt, and I sure as fuck didn't try to collect on it. It would kill my father to know how his business had affected me over the years, just how many men had stolen what I was too small to defend.

Lorenzo shook me by my hair and dragged me across the floor, scraping my knees across the carpet. "I've been thinking about you." He lifted me by my hair and threw me down on the bed, pressing my stomach against the mattress.

I tried to flail my arms, but he pinned me with his body. The salty smell of stale cologne wrapped around me as I grabbed the sheet in trembling hands. He groaned against me as his hands raced down my sides, pushing my long t-shirt up and exposing my panties. A cold blade trailed along my skin as he cut through the lace. He held the knife to the side of my neck, threatening me into silence. Even if I screamed, it would only bring more Vigliones to the party. When I heard the buckle of his belt come undone, I swallowed hard and reminded myself I wouldn't cry. His fat fingers prodded between my thighs, and I closed my eyes to drown out the light.

"I'll fucking kill you," I hissed with venom in my voice.

"You wish," he said through a lengthy groan that echoed in my mind. "You won't be able to touch me, you bitch." His hot breath brushed against my ear as he fumbled with his dick to position himself behind me.

Oh god, did Enzo send him for me like he promised?

Enzo

WITH HEAVY STEPS, I jogged toward Gia's room in the opposite wing of the house. The air in my lungs caught in my throat, making me exhale sharply. I couldn't believe what I'd seen, what was happening under my own goddamn roof.

I took a deep breath, trying to fill my lungs as I burst through her door. It was dark but I heard rattling and heavy breathing the moment I stepped through the doorway. I was surprised I could hear anything at all over the whoosh of my blood in my ears. My hand raced for the light switch and flipped it on, illuminating the room and exposing Gia's precarious situation.

Lorenzo's pants were half off, his hips pressed tight

against her ass. It made my blood run hot, nearly burning me. She hardly made a peep beneath his upper body, which held her down and pushed her into the mattress. For a moment, I couldn't help but wonder if she was a willing participant beneath him. *Not Gia.* I shook that thought away, knowing exactly what kind of girl she was. She'd rip his dick off and choke him with it if she could.

I grabbed Lorenzo by the collar of his suit and ripped him backward. He stumbled and tried to reach for his undone pants. I looked over at Gia. She held her hand against her neck, blood dripping from where the knife had nicked her. Drops of crimson trailed down her skin and stained the sheets as she reached for her shirt and pulled it down, trying to cover herself. She sat up and drew her legs into her chest. My face flushed at the sight of her reddened cheeks and the fear in her eyes. As much as I loved that look on her pretty face, I only liked it if it was me who caused it.

I lifted the hem of my white sleeveless shirt and instinctively reached for my gun. My hands grasped at nothingness on the waistline of my gray sweatpants, and I realized I'd left it back in my room. Once I saw what was happening on that camera, I had to get to her.

My eyes narrowed at Lorenzo. "What the fuck are you doing?"

"Chill, Enzo." Lorenzo buckled his pants and puffed his chest at me, chuckling to himself as he looked down at her.

"We don't fucking rape in this family." I pushed him backward, knowing my words in front of Gia were a lie. We walked that line in this family, and I wasn't proud of it. What I meant to say was we don't rape Gia. Period. If I couldn't, no one fucking could.

"You don't even know what we do in this family!" Lorenzo barked back, grabbing me by my shirt.

He's got a point there. I don't wanna know nothing about those types of deals. "I know we offered Gia protection while she was here. Ask your brother!"

"Silvio? Who do you think gave me his blessing on this? I don't step out of my position without being told to do so." Lorenzo laughed as he pushed me away from him. "Back down, Enzo, and let me finish what I started."

I drew my arm back and punched Lorenzo in the face. His nose crunched beneath my fist. "I may have been named after you, but we ain't nothing alike." I landed another strike to Lorenzo's face, and he cupped his nose. Blood trailed through his fingers and dripped onto his suit, staining it a dark crimson. He fell against the wall, knocking a hole in the drywall with his elbow. "Get the fuck out of my sight," I said, raising my voice and pointing toward the door.

Lorenzo stared at me, still holding his nose to try to stop the bleeding. He squinted his eyes before looking down at Gia. "This isn't over."

"Now! Get the fuck outta here!"

The strength in my voice startled Gia, and she clutched her knees tighter.

"You're lucky I didn't have my gun, Enzo. I didn't want the bitch to get her hands on it." He gestured toward her with his chin.

"Wise move." Gia would have shot the shit out of him without losing a wink of sleep. She was savage, and it was what I loved most about her. Besides that perfect fucking ass of hers. I pushed Lorenzo a final time. "You're right about one thing, though. This isn't over."

"Really? You gonna take the side of some broad over your family? She's a goddamn dog. A fucking Silvani. She's only good for one thing." He cupped his crotch in a crude gesture.

I inhaled, drawing as much air into my lungs as I could to control the tremble in my lip. My muscles tensed and flexed beneath my shirt. Lorenzo knew I was a force to be reckoned with, even if I wasn't as tall as he was, and he eyed me as if sizing me up, as if trying to figure out if Gia's pussy was worth more of a fight.

It is.

"If you don't fucking leave now, Lorenzo, I swear to my mother, I'll hang you from the balcony by your goddamn neck!"

"Eh, yeah, I'm going." He lifted his hands defensively. Lorenzo's steps receded after he slammed the door behind him. The picture frames rattled on the wall from the force.

My attention turned toward Gia, my eyes roving over her. The corners of her mouth were drawn downward, her lips tight. She stared at me with a look of well-deserved accusation plastered across her face.

"Gia . . ." I tried to sit beside her, but she scooted away from me.

"You really did it, didn't you?" she snapped.

"That? You think I had anything to do with that?" My eyes softened for a moment.

"Didn't you? You threatened it . . ." Her voice lost its momentum, trailing off at the end.

My shoulders fell forward. If anyone was going to get in Gia's pants, it would be me, not my fucking uncle. The timing of the threat was just a poor coincidence. "That was *never* supposed to happen." When I reached my hand out to touch her arm, she pulled it away from me. "He didn't . . . did he?"

"Why the fuck do you care?" she asked, finding the power of her voice again.

My eyes darted. I wanted to say more, I should have said more, but I couldn't bring myself to speak those words. I rubbed my hand over my mouth and let it wipe down my beard. An audible exhale slipped past my lips. "I can't apologize enough for this, Gia," I said as I stood and put my hands on my hips.

Her body trembled, and her hands scrambled for a blanket as if she couldn't pull enough fabric over her. "I don't believe a word you say. You're just like the rest of them. I thought for a moment, for a single moment last night, that you were different."

"Of course I'm not different. Are you different from your father?"

"My family doesn't use their dicks as weapons!" She sat taller and stared at me. "Please enlighten me. How was what he did any different from what you threatened me with last night?"

"You don't understand."

"Oh, I understand just fine. You're a family of fucking pigs, and you have the nerve to call me a dog. At least you can share a home with a goddamn dog." She stood, tossed the blanket aside, and squared off to me. My muscles tensed as I looked down at her.

"I don't know how I can prove I had nothing to do with this." I reached out and grabbed her arms, holding them at her sides. Her muscles trembled as if she was ready to sock me in the mouth again. My touch made her flinch as I brushed a lock of sweaty hair out of her face. "I'll figure out how to prove it to you, but I'm not leaving you here alone."

I looked around the room and spotted her bag. She shifted her weight as I dug through it, my hands racing through the fabric, lifting random articles of clothing and tossing them aside. I threw a pair of shorts to her, and she slipped them on without looking at me.

"Come on," I commanded as I grabbed her arm and dragged her into the hallway.

"Where are we going?" she asked, digging her heels into the ground.

"My room."

Chapter Thirteen

Enzo

My heart raced in my chest as I brought Gia toward my section of the house. It was somewhere no woman had seen outside of the family, but here I was, bringing an enemy into my den. Her light footsteps shuffled along the carpeted floor leading to my bedroom. She looked around at the walls in the hallway, made of wooden squares intricately carved into an interlocking pattern. Lights hung from the ceiling, dotting the path toward my room. I'd left the double door open in my haste to get to her, and the camera view was still open on my phone on the pillow. Her bed was clearly visible on the screen, and her blanket was still strewn on the ground from her assault. I grabbed it before she could see it.

She looked around with wide eyes. My room was as big as some people's homes. The moonlight spread across a large, multi-paneled picture window. Beside it, a door led to the balcony overlooking the property. Her eyes landed on the pool table and her shoulders relaxed a bit.

"Really? A pool table? Do you even know how to play?" she said with a snarky tone I didn't appreciate. She knew very little about me.

"Actually, I used to be quite good. I even made it to the semi-finals in a tournament in Las Vegas." I puffed my chest a bit, the corners of my mouth rising slightly.

I walked to my bed and grabbed the black .357 revolver off the bedside table. Gia looked at me with tight lips as I put it down the back of my waistband. Most people in our business shied away from revolvers, but I loved them. I was accurate, making every bullet count, and there were no casings to leave behind. That gun had been my best friend.

My block-headed rottweiler leapt from the floor beside my bed when he heard us come in. He charged toward Gia, who showed no fear at the giant beast barreling toward her. Her eyes lit up as she knelt and allowed my dog to tackle her. He licked her face, his big pink tongue lolling from his mouth as he sat and stared at me. I reached down and rubbed his head.

"What's his name?" she asked, pulling herself back to her knees.

"Atheist." I rubbed my hand through my hair.

"Really?" As she rose to her feet, Atheist wagged his nub of a tail, his big, meaty body wiggling with excitement.

"He's a guard dog." I smirked at her.

"Clearly," she said as she wiped the drool off her face.

"Why don't you take the bed? Try to get some sleep." I looked at the overstuffed armchair and the couch, knowing I had plenty of other places to lie down. Not that I'd be able to sleep. Atheist hopped onto the chair. *Couch it is.*

Gia blinked at me for several moments before turning toward my bed. She peeled the blanket back and looked at the mattress with noticeable hesitation before cautiously climbing onto it as if she were crawling into a fire. Atheist lifted his head and hopped down from the chair, leaping onto the bed and pressing his body into her, protecting her. A smile crept across my face as I fluffed a pillow and lay on the couch.

I kicked off my shoes and stared up at the ceiling fan. My thoughts raced faster than the blades spinning above my head. *Did Silvio really allow and encourage what Lorenzo tried to do?* I wasn't naïve. I knew the men of my family were no strangers to sexual assault. Women were a plaything. That was how I grew up. I wasn't the kindest to women, but Gia was different. *She ain't gonna forgive me for this one.* I sighed as I looked over at her, her arm wrapped around Atheist, a soft snore coming from the bed. *What do I do about Lorenzo?* I rubbed my forehead at the thought because I knew what had to be done.

"Enzo?" a small, tired voice said from the bed, and I realized the snores had come from Atheist.

"Yeah?"

"You stopped him in time," she said so softly I almost didn't hear her over the buzz of the fan. I blew out a breath and rubbed my temples.

"You weren't even scared of him? I ain't ever seen a girl so calm."

"I'm a Silvani. You think this was my first rodeo? Shit, it's probably not even my last." She turned over and stared at me.

"How many times?" I asked, unsure if I even wanted to know the answer.

"How many times, or how many men?" she said with a sadness in her voice that I could feel from the couch. "Too many."

"And I . . ." My voice trailed off, unable to complete my

sentence as shame burned a hole in my gut. I cringed, recalling how I'd tried to force her, even if it was just to scare her a bit.

"Hey, it's fine. Really. Such is this life." Her lips pushed into a pout as her eyes stared ahead, locked in her memories. Even through her strength, I knew she wasn't fine. I felt the intense desire to go to her side and kiss her, to comfort her the only way I knew how.

Have you ever wanted someone so badly you can almost taste them on your tongue? I bit my lip. *Not this way.*

"I didn't have anything to do with this. You know that, right?" I said, covering my crotch with a pillow to hide my unintentional excitement.

"I don't. I don't trust you," she said with no emotion. This was merely a state of being for her.

"Give me a bit, Giovanna. I'll show you." I put my arm behind my head and exhaled. She didn't speak, but why should she have believed me? I was a Viglione.

"Yeah, yeah." She sounded drowsy.

Atheist stood and walked in a tight circle before plopping down on the bed again. I looked at her, her eyes closed, her lips loose.

I know what I have to do.

Chapter Fourteen

Gia

The clouds hung above us as we walked toward the woods on their property. Going into the cover of the trees with a Viglione was a terrible fucking idea. He could be taking me to assault me or murder me. Who the hell knew with him? I dragged my feet across the forest floor as birds flew to the ground, pecking at the earth muddied by the recent rain.

"Where are we going?" I said, a bit more petulant than I meant.

"Stop whining, will you? We got a little ways to go." Every tense muscle in his rigid body flexed. He had a gun tucked into his waistband, different from the one I saw in the bedroom, and I envisioned grabbing it off him with every step he took.

He wiped his hand through his hair, which he always did when he was nervous, and I finally grabbed his sleeve and made him stop walking.

"What's your problem?" I asked with my hands crossed over my chest. Another petulant gesture.

"You'll see in a minute," he said with a hardened glare.

We walked deeper into the woods until we were surrounded by towering trees. The leaves shook and sent leftover droplets onto our bare skin. I bumped into Enzo when he stopped while I was still admiring the scenery, and my gaze landed on something I enjoyed much more than the trees.

Lying in front of us was Lorenzo, bound and gagged. Dried blood mixed with fresh streams as it flowed down his face. He was soaked from head to toe, shivering in a ribbed sleeveless shirt and boxers. Water and dirt mixed with his graying hair to create thick mats. He screamed, though it was muffled by the thick black fabric wrapped around his mouth. Water dripped from the tip of his nose as he thrashed on the ground.

I stared down at him with wide eyes, his piercing gaze locked on me as Enzo lifted him onto his knees. The gag fell to the ground once Enzo untied it from the back of his head.

"Are you fucking kidding me, Enzo?" he screamed, coughing up blood. The crimson stained his skin and shirt, mixing with the wet mud caked on his clothes.

"I am not." Enzo smirked and squatted beside him.

Lorenzo strained against his restraints as he tried to get to Enzo, but the furious attempt didn't faze him. He almost seemed to find amusement in it.

Lorenzo changed tactics. "Boss, I was just trying to have a little fun with her," he said with a humorless laugh.

"Did you have fun, Gia? Was it fun for you?" Enzo turned his face toward me.

"No," I said with a shake of my head.

"What bothers me, Lorenzo, is that we disowned you once. You came crawling back, asking for another chance. I let you work for me, against my better judgment. My jobs kept you fed, yet you had the nerve to step in on my affairs."

"But—" Lorenzo shook his head and drew his lips in.

"There's nothing to 'but' about. I told you she was off limits, that she was my responsibility, and you disrespected not only her, but me!"

Enzo reached into the back of his dress pants and grabbed his pistol, wrapping his hand around the wooden grip. He threaded a silencer onto the barrel before holding the gun toward me. I stared at the cold steel in his grasp, too wary to step forward and take it from him. Noticing my apprehension, he stood, took several steps toward me, and shoved the pistol into my hand. Compared to my pistol— which was easy to conceal just about anywhere—this intimidating gun had some serious weight to it. *Is he really trusting me with a pistol right now? After everything that happened?* I felt the familiar pang of nervous excitement as I wrapped my hand around the metal and racked the slide. A gun in my hand always made me feel like I held all the power, and right then, I did.

"What is all this?" I asked.

"Retribution," Enzo said with a cold expression.

That was such a beautiful fucking word.

I looked beyond Enzo and stared at the man sobbing in front of us. "You sure?" I asked one more time.

"I won't tolerate rape. I'm not like him or Silvio," Enzo said with a snarl. I didn't quite believe him because I'd heard too many stories to convince me otherwise.

He grabbed my waist and led me behind Lorenzo. His desperate pleas quickly became annoying, the sounds gnawing into my ears, making me want to silence them that much more.

"I said I'd fucking kill you, didn't I?" I said with a suave confidence that invigorated me. "What was it that you said? That I couldn't touch you?"

The silencer's cool metal pressed against the back of his head as he sobbed through prayers. I looked at Enzo one more time, giving him a final chance to stop me. When his lips merely pursed, I turned my attention back to Lorenzo. He wasn't just a man who tried to rape me. He was the embodiment of *every* man who had.

This was something I was raised to love and hate—the moment where I took a life, even if it was a deserved execution. My finger was steadfast on the trigger as I curled it toward me. The unmistakable sound of a silenced firearm pierced through the air, cutting off Lorenzo's screaming and praying. He fell forward, crumpling into a limp pile. Rich red blood flowed from his head wound, poured onto the ground, and saturated the earth.

That was the part I hated. The moment after my victim took their last breath. The uncomfortable silence of murder.

Enzo snuck up behind me and wrapped his hand around the still-smoking pistol. He pulled it away from me, as if I might take aim at him next.

"See, Gia? I had nothing to do with it," Enzo said with his body still pressed against mine.

"Enzo," I said, my gaze on Lorenzo's body. "We just killed a member of your family. Your father's goddamn brother. How do we—"

"Lorenzo had enough enemies, so nobody will be surprised he went missing." Enzo looked down at the body. "And I'll make sure he stays missing."

"Pretty ballsy to trust me with your gun," I said with a smirk.

"Sometimes you gotta go toe to toe with a lioness and hope she doesn't bite ya," he said as he unthreaded the silencer and pocketed it. "Plus, there was only one bullet. Had I given you the choice between me and him, you'd have made the right choice." He smirked and tilted his head, which annoyed me because it made him irresistible for a moment.

There was an uncomfortable excitement between my legs as he stared back at me. *What's wrong with me?*

<hr>

Enzo

*W*ELL, *there's no taking that back,* I thought as we walked toward the house. The pistol stabbed me in the lower back. It was much clunkier than my revolver, but I'd needed to use a silencer so no one would hear the shot. Gia stayed silent behind me, which was unusual for her. She was *never* quiet. When I looked back, she had her arms crossed and her gaze fixated on the ground in front of her.

"You okay?" I asked, and her dark eyes finally met mine.

"Fine," she said without a hint of emotion.

"You don't seem fine," I prodded. I didn't know why I gave a shit about how she felt. It was done.

"You don't know me, Enzo."

That's where she was wrong. I knew her more than she knew herself.

I turned on my heels and stopped in front of her. "If I

knew this was gonna upset you so much, I wouldn't have let you kill him."

"You think that's what I'm upset about? You *really* don't know me like you think you do." She flashed a dark smile, and I couldn't help but let my own lips creep into one as well.

I tapped my foot on the ground. "I'll bite. What is it, then?"

"None of your business," she muttered.

"Alright, suit yourself." I turned around and kept walking toward the house. I wouldn't argue with her or play these pathetic little games. If she wanted to talk, she knew where to find me.

We remained quiet for the rest of the walk, with only the sound of rustling bushes and chirping birds to break up the silence. I opened the back door for her, and she rolled her eyes at me.

"You're welcome," I quipped as she pushed past me.

Once we were back in my room, she looked down at the blood splatter on her hand. The wind was not your friend during an execution. I should have thought that through. I gestured toward the bathroom. She hurried inside, and the water began to run before the door even closed. She couldn't wait a moment longer to get the blood off her skin.

I slipped off my muddy shoes and sat on the couch. The leather molded around my body and welcomed me. I let out a sigh, leaned back, and laced my hands behind my head, closing my eyes for mere moments before the bathroom door creaked open. I kept my eyes shut and didn't react until the feel of her fingers on my belt buckle demanded my attention. I sat up and looked into Gia's hungry eyes. She seemed like she was starving for me and I wanted to feed her, let her devour me, but . . . Ah, it all made sense now.

"Girl, you definitely are Cosa Nostra," I groaned.

"How so?" She stopped her assault on my buckle and stared at me.

"We just murdered someone, and your pussy is wet, am I right?"

She squinted her eyes as if she realized what my words meant. With a sigh, she sat beside me on the couch.

I turned toward her. "It's not a bad thing, babygirl. We ain't wired right. If we were, we wouldn't be in this business in the first place."

"Eh, I'm better than this," she said with a drop of her shoulders.

Goddamn it, I cursed to myself. *So close.* I shouldn't have stopped her. She could have had her moment of realization later, after I'd spilled my come down her throat.

Atheist ran over and threw his huge body between us, drool dripping from his jowls. Gia rubbed his body, resting her head against him.

"It doesn't bother you that I'm the reason your uncle is dead?" Her voice was low and insecure. Again, nothing like my Gia.

"Lorenzo is the reason Lorenzo is dead, not you," I said with a dismissive wave of my hand.

"But if I wasn't here—"

"He'd still have done something to piss me off sooner or later. Lorenzo's had a bullet with his name on it ever since he came back to us."

"What happened with that, anyway?" she asked as she drew her legs toward her chest.

"Drugs." I shook my head. "We don't fuck with drugs. Not at that volume. The feds were sniffing his ass, so he tucked his tail and came back for protection."

"Lotta good that did," Gia said with a pained smile.

"You guys didn't worry about the drug trail leading back to you?"

"Nah. Well, I did, but Silvio said, 'He's family!' and let the motherfucker back in." I shook my head again. Silvio was the most reckless and selfish leader. He didn't think before he did a damn thing, and this business ran poorly on goddamn whims. We needed cool, calculated, and methodical responses to everything. Anything else would be like going into a board meeting with a fucking pigeon in your briefcase—useless for anything other than drawing attention where it shouldn't be drawn.

"Why don't you call him dad?"

She asked a question I never wanted to answer. Every family had dark secrets, and we weren't no different, but I planned to die with mine. Bring that shit right to the goddamn grave with me. I looked at Atheist, the only breathing thing I'd told my secrets to, and patted him. He wouldn't judge me, unlike people. Even a person like Gia.

"I just don't."

"That's not why," she prodded, her eyebrows furrowed.

I blinked at her, memories racing through my head. I swallowed hard, though I tried not to show it. Silvio was capable of all sorts of cruelty until I was old enough to fight back. I missed too much school and had to drop out before I could even make it past the eighth grade because of the beatings. He would get off on me fucking his whores when I was hardly old enough to know what I was doing. That hardly scratched the surface of his cruelty. It was no wonder I became the way I did. When I was sixteen, I finally found my voice and strength. I pulled a pistol on him. Told him I'd had enough.

But I couldn't tell Gia any of that.

"Silvio did some real terrible things to me when I was

growing up. Things you don't talk about." That was all she would get out of me.

"Enzo . . ." she said with sympathy I didn't want from anybody, especially her. If she knew all the things he'd done to me or made me do, she wouldn't sit beside me.

"Nah, it's fine. How do you say it? Such is this life?" I rubbed my hands down my pants and avoided her gaze. Feeling vulnerable in any capacity filled me with an anger that rose from the bitter hurt I still carried.

"That's different. Shit's not supposed to come from the inside." She pursed her lips.

I cleared my throat to break the heavy silence between us.

Gia pushed Atheist off the couch and crawled over to me. She straddled my waist and looked down at me with her rich brown eyes. I pushed the hair off her shoulder and pulled her close to me as I kissed the soft skin of her neck. She sure knew how to calm the beast inside me. She put the goddamn thing to sleep. My hands raced down her sides as she started to remove her shirt.

I'll regret this later, I told myself as I put my hands over hers and stopped her, leaving a sliver of tan skin exposed on her stomach. Her face twisted in a clear expression of frustration. *Ain't no one likes to be rejected.*

"Why?" she asked with a deep sigh.

The truth? The thoughts of my past and my childhood couldn't have been more of a turn off. Even with Gia's warmth on my lap, I couldn't break away from my memories. If I was going to fuck her, I'd need to have a clear head. Or at least one that wasn't quite so heavy.

The twist in her expression rubbed me all the wrong ways.

"You don't get to decide when I fuck you," I snapped and pushed her off my lap.

She sat on the couch with a huff. "Whatever, you dick," she said as she tugged down her shirt. "Your loss."

Oh, I know.

Chapter Fifteen

Gia

A loud bang woke me up, something that would startle any one of us in this life. I rose onto my elbows and looked toward the window. I groaned as I stared at Enzo. A cigarette dangled from his lips as he leaned over the pool table. Smoke rose and his mouth pursed around it. "Did I wake you?" he asked, though he knew the answer. "Do you wanna play?"

I looked at the clock beside the bed. "It's three in the morning. No. Fuck right off." I rolled over and covered my head with the blanket.

His smooth voice wafted over to me. "I really would like you to come play with me. I can't sleep." Another drive of the cue ball caused a clattering roar as balls scattered everywhere.

Goddamn it. I sat up with a groan and peeled myself out of sleep's warm embrace. I rubbed my eyes as I walked over and leaned against the pool table. Striped and solid balls dotted the table's felt surface. Enzo drew the stick back and hit the cue ball, knocking two striped balls into two different pockets. My mouth dropped. He removed his cigarette from his mouth just long enough to have a drawn-out sip of beer.

"Do you know how to play?" he asked as he handed the stick to me.

"Yeah, no. These aren't the sticks I'm familiar with." I chuckled at my own joke, but his lips didn't even twitch. I cleared my throat nervously. "No, I don't know how to play."

He kept his gaze on the balls as he planted himself behind me. I leaned my upper body toward the table. I knew that much, at least. Enzo guided my hands as he tried to show me how to strike the cue ball and aim it. He might as well have been trying to teach me Spanish. When I went to strike the ball, the stick skidded along the tabletop and barely tapped the ball, moving it merely a few inches.

He exhaled as he patiently tried to line me up for the next shot, the smoke from his cigarette playing in the air between us. My hips grinded into him as he pressed his body against me.

"I know what you're doing." He smirked, the cigarette dangling between his loose lips. "I ain't ever moved my hips like that to play pool."

My cheeks flushed with heat, and I halted the movement of my hips as I tried to strike the ball. Once again, I missed it.

He turned me to face him and exhaled smoke into my face. "You aren't any good at this."

"I never said I was." My lips pouted, and my eyes scanned down his body, hovering at the outline of his cock beneath his gray sweatpants. He was hard, tenting the fabric of his pants. I don't know what came over me, but I wanted him so goddamn bad I could taste him. Saying no to me earlier made this a challenge, and I wanted to conquer it. "Can't we stop being enemies for one night?" I asked with an ache between my legs. Fuck Enzo. I mean, truly. Fuck him in every sense of the word. I equally hated and wanted him inside me.

"You ain't ever been my enemy, Giovanna Silvani." He tossed the pool stick to the ground, and his warm hand wrapped around my throat in a somewhat tender way—for a Viglione, at least. His other hand brushed my hair from my face. "But I don't know if I want to give you what you want yet."

"Goddamn it, Enzo, please." Frustration and a hint of desperation laced my words. I hated how I sounded, but I *needed* him.

"Babygirl," he whispered as he grabbed my cheek.

"Don't say sweet shit to me." I pushed at his chest, my annoyance boiling over.

He fisted a chunk of my hair as he worked his sweatpants down with his other hand. My eyes widened at the sight of him, and I bit my lip. Like everything else on Enzo, physically, he was perfect. Emotionally? That was something else entirely.

"How about this? You give me that pretty mouth of yours, and I'll show you what hell tastes like. Then you can decide if you want to walk through fire with me." He craned my neck.

Before he even finished his sentence, I had dropped to my knees, the carpet rough against my bare skin. *Fire? I'd let him set me alight right now if it meant I could feel him inside me.* My lip trembled as he stroked himself in front of my face. I hesitated. Not because I didn't want it, but because of how fucking bad I *did* want it. It was gross how much I wanted to make him come.

"I guess not," he said as he moved to lift his pants.

"No, no, wait." I reached for the fabric and held it down, swatting his hand away.

He brushed my hair out of my face and balled it behind my head. I leaned into him, slowly licking up his length, cock-teasing him the way he'd teased me. He groaned at the warmth of my tongue on him, and a growl formed low in his throat as he pushed himself into my mouth, unable to wait one more moment to be inside it. It was the first time he ever felt my mouth, and I wondered if I had been worth all that waiting. His deep groan the moment I wrapped my mouth around him answered my question. He looked down at me with intense blue eyes, and it made me weak. Had I not been on my knees already, I wouldn't have been able to stay on my feet.

His hand guided my motions from behind my head, faster and rougher each time. He thrust his hips forward, forcing me to take more of him until I gagged. He pulled out long enough for me to wipe the drool from my chin before he shoved me back on him. He fucked my mouth so carelessly, and I swam with curiosity about just how good he'd feel inside me.

"Fuck," he whispered as he dragged me to my feet. He looked down at me with hunger, wiping his thumb along my lower lip. "Goddamn it, Gia."

I knew what I wanted, and if I got him going enough, he'd give it to me. My hands trembled as I lifted my t-shirt over my head. My hair tumbled over my shoulders. Enzo stared at me, his gaze boring through me as his hands dropped to my breasts. He caressed them roughly and kissed me. The taste of his cock was still on my lips. I moaned at his touch. Every grip of his fingers was rough, like that was all I was to him. That's all I wanted it to be, too. I wanted to be used.

By him.

He grabbed the back of his shirt and pulled it off, tossing it to the ground. Now I was the one doing the staring as his taut muscles rippled beneath tanned skin, his posture still tense and rigid. He wouldn't relax, not until he got what he wanted. What I needed him to take.

Enzo grabbed my hips and turned me around, bending me over the pool table. My breasts pressed against the cold wood, making me shiver. His hands grasped the waistband of my shorts as he pulled them down with a harsh motion I'd only dreamed of before that moment. They fell to the floor, and I kicked them away. His hands raced along my back and over the curves of my ass.

"Just for one night," he whispered in my ear before devouring the skin of my neck.

I nodded. One night. One evening where there was no line in the sand between our families. Not until the tide receded and divided us all over again.

He pushed himself inside me as if he were too hungry to wait any longer. His cock stretched me, and I worried I'd tear from his hurried thrusts. I whimpered as I dropped my head toward the table.

Enzo stopped and reached for my shoulder. "You okay?"

"Yes, it's just been a while," I told him through heavy breaths painted with pain and the hopes of pleasure.

"Do you want me to go easy?" he asked as he brushed my hair over my shoulder, his fingers grazing the skin between my shoulder blades.

"No," I panted.

His hands found their home on my hips again, and he

pushed into me with a hint of hesitation before every thrust. I knew he was trying not to hurt me, so I pushed against him, forcing him to go deeper. He took the hint, grabbing my shoulders and fucking me harder, the hesitation disappearing with every thrust. He was eating me alive and I wanted to give him every last piece of me.

"Enzo," I moaned as his pool table shook from his strength behind me. "Talk dirty to me," I whispered.

"You have an incredible pussy," he groaned.

"No . . . degrade me," I said.

He stopped for a moment. His hands raced down my back while he contemplated my request, his cock still throbbing inside me. He pulled out of me and turned me around to face him.

"There's only one thing the Silvani daughter is good for," he whispered. He forced me back to my knees and pushed his cock into my mouth. I tasted my sweet excitement on him. "And that's to take a dick like this. In your dirty fucking mouth." He shoved his cock so far down my throat I thought I'd swallow him.

I gagged, trying to fight back the bile that teased the top of my stomach. My eyes watered, tears falling against my will. He pulled himself from my throat and let me pant in front of him.

"Tell me what you are, Giovanna," he commanded.

"I'm a dirty whore who's only good for one thing. Sucking your cock."

"I know you want more, desperate fucking Silvani," he growled. "You don't deserve my cock but if I bend you over, I can almost forget that you're Gia Silvani. I can almost pretend you're someone worth my come." He lifted me by my hair and bent me over. "But I fucking want to fill something up, and what better than Sylvester's daughter? His sweet little girl is my goddamn whore. When was the last time you were fucked, Gia? I bet it's been a while. You're a frigid bitch that no one's willing to get close to."

I swallowed hard as his words struck deeper than I expected. Because he was right. People in the business thought I was frigid. Cold as ice. That was how I survived.

He pushed his cock inside me.

"I'm a useless whore," I whispered. I moaned as he talked down to me. He wasn't the only one with a messed-up childhood.

"Not totally useless, Silvani. You have an incredible mouth and pussy. But that's it. Good to use, but there's nothing else worthwhile about you. Is there, Gia?" Enzo's thrusts hastened, going harder, as if he began to believe the words coming out of his mouth.

I shook my head and fought back tears. Getting upset over it somehow made me clench around him. All the times men had taken me and whispered such shit in my ears.

Good for nothing more than paying your daddy's debt.

Stop talking. Your mouth is only good for one thing.

Will your daddy's heart break when he sees the pictures of us fucking you?

Enzo lifted my upper body, grabbing my chest with his strong hands. He turned my face toward him with a rough grasp. When he saw the tear that fell from the corner of my eye, I knew he'd stop. He wouldn't understand that my tears meant to keep going. What made me cry also made me come.

"Gotta be honest, Gia, I don't wanna talk to you like that right now." He kissed my neck. "I've wanted you for so long, ever since that night on the balcony." He rocked his pelvis in shallow strokes that made my body tremble. "I know you like it. Every word that's meant to hurt you makes your pussy clench around me. I promise I'll talk dirty all you want . . . after tonight." He bit down on my shoulder. "I'll tell you how you're a desperate *whore* who begged me to fuck her . . . tomorrow."

He pulled out and turned me around, picking me up and placing me on the edge of the pool table. I wrapped my legs around his waist. Enzo stroked himself for a moment, his cock drenched with my excitement, before pushing himself back inside me. I gasped at the angle, a perfect tilt upward that rubbed against everything in all the right ways. The table rocked as he grabbed my shoulders and slammed into me. He leaned forward and devoured my chest, his mouth roving over every inch of my breasts. His tongue swirled along my nipples, and the sensations were almost too much.

His thrusts quickened as he buried his face in my neck. The fire lit inside me, the soft hairs of his pelvis rubbing my clit with every movement of his hips. As I tensed against him, he groaned my name and rubbed between my legs. His touch was electric.

"You can come, babygirl," he whispered as he slid his fingers along the slick skin surrounding my clit.

The way he said those words, as if God graced them himself, rippled through me and pushed me over the edge I'd been teetering on. My legs pulled him into me as I shuddered against him, wanting every inch of him.

"Goddamn, Gia," he groaned, holding himself deep inside me as he twitched within me. I spasmed around his cock, squeezing every drop of come from him. His body collapsed against mine, and he kissed me with unstifled passion, as if he hadn't been denying me this since I got here. "Just for tonight? Okay?" he whispered as he drew his mouth away from me.

Chapter Sixteen

Enzo

Silvio was coming home from his business trip, so I woke up on edge. I slid my hands down my sides to smooth the wrinkles in my purple dress shirt. My fingers brushed through my dark hair as I gave myself a final glance in the mirror. When I walked back into my bedroom, Gia was still asleep, wrapped in my blanket. Waking up beside her was something I could get used to. But I absolutely fucking wouldn't. We couldn't play house when we were both at war.

The memory foam mattress sank under my weight when I sat on the bed. "Hey." I rested a hand on her, but she didn't stir. "Gia!" I shook her shoulder, and she finally opened her eyes.

"What?" she groaned.

"We got a job to do," I told her as I grabbed the blanket and peeled it away from her. The corners of my mouth crept upward as I looked at her in my t-shirt.

"What job?" She rubbed her eyes and leaned on her elbow.

"There's some business we gotta take care of."

"That sounds like a you problem," she said as she dropped her head onto the pillow again.

"Silvio's back home, and I ain't leaving you here. Let's go." I tugged her arm. She was delusional if she thought I'd leave her alone with Silvio. He wanted her, maybe even more than I did, as unbelievable as that seemed. I wanted Gia because I *wanted* Gia. Silvio would take Gia because she was a trophy notch to add to his bedpost. Fucking Sylvester's daughter would make him come harder than he ever had. *I ain't leaving her here.* I would carry her ass out if I had to. I cleared my throat.

She groaned and dragged herself out of bed. "Fine, but I'm going to shower first. Can you get my bag?"

"Already did." I gestured toward her bag on the floor. "I also brought you something nice to wear. Can't look like a bum during business hours." I cocked a half smile, and she huffed at me as she walked into the bathroom and slammed the door.

The water turned on, and my curiosity became too much to handle. I grabbed the clothes I'd chosen for her on my way to the bathroom. Steam hit me in the face as I cracked open the door. I stared at her body through the shower's fogged glass. Several showerheads rained hot water down on her, and intricately detailed marble walls surrounded her on nearly every side. I saw the curves of her body, every arch and contour, and I hardened like a motherfucker. My cock strained against my zipper, and I adjusted myself. I placed the outfit on the white marble countertop.

"Can I help you, Enzo?" Her voice was soft but rife with annoyance.

"You don't need to do a damn thing." I smirked, watching her clear an area of fog off the door.

"You're being a creep." She grabbed one of the shower heads and sent a jet of water over the door. The droplets assaulted my shirt, which had been finely pressed.

"Not okay, Gia!" I yelled as I took a step back, stifling a hint of laughter. I cleared my throat and tightened my lips again.

"If you hadn't been in such a rush to get dressed, you could have joined me." The sultry way she spoke hung in the air between us.

Not now, I told myself as I adjusted the collar of my shirt. If I didn't leave the room then, I'd grant her that wish and tease the fuck out of her. The thought of her naked body, slick and wet with water . . . My cock was going to fucking explode if I didn't get out of there. Against my body's will, I left her alone in the bathroom.

I sat on the bed with a sigh and thought about last night. My eyes closed as I imagined how Gia felt. I'd waited so long to sink into her again, yet the moment I was inside her, I realized how much my body remembered hers. It was as if so many years hadn't stretched out between us, because she felt familiar as fuck. My dream couldn't even compare to the real thing. She felt goddamn virginal, and I wanted nothing more than to fill her up and remind her who she really belonged to. She could fight it all she wanted, but her ass was mine. She gripped my dick so hard that it drove me mad. Her body trembled from pleasure, and I wanted to be the one to make her come again. It just wouldn't be so easy for her next time. *That damn woman.* I shook my head. She liked to be degraded, but I'd show her the other ways I could fuck with her pretty little mind.

When I heard the bathroom door open, I sat up tall,

suddenly pulled from my memory. My eyes widened and roamed over her body, and she looked at me with displeasure as she crossed her arms over her chest, overly exposed by the plunging neckline. Her breasts were pushed together, full mounds beneath the thin fabric. The jet-black dress pants hugged her hips, accentuating them.

"I look like a whore." She frowned.

Actually, she did. She looked like a good ol' doll, and it made me want to bend her over and tear those pants off her.

"Nah, not really, no." I chuckled as I stood and stepped toward her. Her eyes narrowed at me, halting my steps. "You look—"

"Forget about it." She dismissed me, her accent suddenly very apparent. She went New York on me, and it made my dick twitch.

"You'll fit in fine. Come on," I demanded.

With a huff, she rifled through her bag before stepping into her heels by the door and following me out of my room.

"Where are we going?" she demanded as I opened the door to the attached underground garage. I unlocked my car, a beep echoing off the damp concrete walls. She climbed into the passenger side of the BMW and stared at me. "Well?"

"A strip club," I said as I put the car into drive, pushing the overhead button for the garage door.

"I'll fit right in, eh?" She furrowed her brow and crossed her arms over her chest, clearly insulted.

"Yeah, you will, but the strippers ain't dressed like you, baby doll." I smirked.

The drive to the club was silent, which was unusual for Gia. The only other time she was that silent was after the execution, and I wondered how she felt about last night. If we both meant what we said about it just being for one night. Just as she was about to speak, I pulled into the parking lot of the large brick building. She tightened her lips and halted her words, her eyes darting around the property.

I parked and stepped out of the car, squinting at the sun as I peered over the roof at the flashing sign that read Toys-n-Dolls. *No one thought that name through.* I laughed when I remembered all the times moms in minivans pulled into this lot, mistaking it for a toy store. *There ain't those kinds of toys here.*

Gia slammed the car door, and I cocked my head at her as I slipped my keys into my chest pocket.

"Let's go," I said as we walked into the huge double doors blackened with window coverings. Music thumped in my chest the moment I stepped inside, the bass vibrating in my head as I rubbed my temples. I looked back at Gia, who seemed unbothered.

The dancers flocked to me, rubbing their hands along my chest and arms as they walked by. I returned a flirty smile as I headed toward the back of the building. I unlocked the heavy metal door and pulled it open, letting Gia walk ahead of me. The door slammed and muffled the music instantly, as if we'd disappeared into our own little world. We kind of had.

Everyone stopped and stared at me, and most importantly, at Gia. I nodded at the tall man in a suit with eyes full of mistrust.

"Is that a Goddamn Silvani?" The man raised his voice as he gestured a large hand toward her. "Are you outta your mind, Enzo? Bringing a fucking Silvani in here." He looked down at his friends and forced a laugh out of them.

"Mr. Bianchi, with no disrespect, remember whose club you're in." I smiled at him with tight lips. "Bullseye"

Bianchi was a made man, sponsored by my family. By Silvio. He was, for all intents and purposes, untouchable.

"Ah, Enzo." Another man rose to his feet, adjusting the buttons on his suit.

I placed my arm in Gia's. She'd grown quiet behind me. That had to be uncomfortable as fuck. I was sure she'd never walked into a room filled with that much hatred aimed at her in her life. No one liked the Silvanis, but very few made that apparent right in front of them. We stepped toward the table with poker cards laid out on it, and I pulled a chair out for her.

"Kenny." I put my hand out and shook his. Kenny Agostino was about my age, the eldest son in the Agostino family. We grew up together. Our families intertwined before we were even born. Silvio had fucked his mother, and you don't fuck another man's wife in this business. If anyone found out, our alliance would die faster than Bullseye's victims.

"Bianchi, as in the East Coast Bianchis?" Gia looked at him with an unwavering glare.

"The one and only." He tipped his hat toward her with fake pleasantry.

"They call you Bullseye, right?" She gestured toward her forehead and mimed a death expression. The men at the table laughed, the corners of even Bullseye's lips rising slightly. "It's an honor, sir." Gia crossed her legs. Bianchi was the one you called to get rid of the people no one else wanted to touch. He was the reaper. "Are we going to play?" She motioned toward the deck of cards, and a slim man in a tan suit picked them up, shuffled them, and started a new deal.

"You playin', boss?" Rudy asked without looking at me, fanning out the cards in his hand.

I shook my head and put a hand over the deck, stopping the man from dealing them. "Ain't no time for cards, boys. We got a problem," I said firmly, getting down to business.

Everyone looked up at me.

"There's a snitch among us." I scanned the room, reading the solemn faces.

Gia's body tensed as my voice hardened and became foreign to her. When it came to business, I was unrecognizable. There was no room for weakness.

"Does someone want to confess to getting involved with the feds? They're opening a goddamn sex trafficking case on this very fucking building." I swept the cards and chips off the table. They crashed to the floor and skittered across the ground. I looked at the two men across from Gia, their expressions cool and confident. My eyes scanned the crowd further, eyeing Bianchi and Agostino and noting the anger on their faces. I looked down at Rudy, who tried to wipe the sweat off his forehead. "Rudy. Dear, sweet Rudy." I leaned over the table, placing my hand near the revolver on my hip.

"I didn't talk to no feds, Enzo." Rudy looked up at me with eyes that were as deceitful as the tone of his voice. He was fucking terrified, and rightfully so. He fucked with my business.

"I don't understand why you'd put your family at risk, Rudes." I stood and circled behind him. Everyone tensed, their hands on their pistols. "You know damn well Silvio will take out that pretty wife of yours if you betray him." Wives and children were supposed to be off limits—it was in our code—but Silvio didn't seem to follow the rules anymore.

Rudy stood with his hands in front of him. "Enzo, I had to. You don't understand. They were sniffin' around my family."

"No, I understand just fine, Rudy. You gotta put your family first. I get that, I do. We're all about protecting our own. Right, boys?"

No one responded.

"Should we even be discussing this around her?" Kenny gestured toward Gia.

"That is my business," I said.

"You're worried about the feds, yet here you are, bringing in a different but equally dangerous enemy into our midst."

"The Silvanis ain't in this business and ain't our competition. Besides, *she's mine*. And I take responsibility for her." I felt the hot stares of the room, especially radiating from behind me, where Gia sat. "Anyway, where were we? Oh right, the feds. What did you tell them?"

Rudy stuttered out a response. "The . . . the feds were hot on our tails for a drug bust that went south."

"Ahh, well, see boys? That's why we don't fuck with drugs, Rudy. None of us want the fucking DEA searching around here, and we definitely don't want the goddamn FB-fucking-I in here either." My hand gripped my revolver so tightly that my knuckles turned white. "What did you tell them?" I enunciated every word, my patience wearing thin.

"Nothin' much, just about the women they were bringing through here sometimes."

I took a deep breath and rubbed my temple, wiping down my face and grazing my beard.

"You know what, it's fine, Rudy, it's fine," I said as he stared at me. Everyone was frozen, knowing damn well that it was not fine. "You leave us to worry about the FBI, and you won't have to worry about nothin'."

I nodded at Bullseye, who swiftly pulled out his pistol and placed a bullet between Rudy's eyes. His body hit the metal chair on the way down as he crumpled onto the concrete floor. Blood pooled from his head, fanning around him in a rich crimson puddle.

"Do we have a fucking understanding about the feds now?" I raised my voice, scanning with my eyes and hovering on every person, including Gia, whose expression was unsurprisingly calm. She was fucking unflappable.

"Now what?" Bullseye asked.

"Get everyone out who wasn't here by choice. I don't care what ya do to them, but they gotta go." I stepped over Rudy's body and sat in his chair. "Play by the books until this investigation is over."

"Do we stop laundering?" Kenny asked, his voice trembling slightly.

"Everything, anything that ain't legal."

"But, boss, that will cost us—" Bullseye began.

"It will cost us a lot more in federal fucking prison than to halt operations for now," I snapped.

"We ceasing operations at the other joints too?" Kenny asked. His concern was the lucrative smoke shop he managed.

"Nah, keep everything else running. Hell, run it harder if you have to," I said as I looked at Gia. "And if she's around, she's an extension of me, do we understand? No one touches her or says fuck all about her family."

The room grew silent as the smell of blood infiltrated the room. Whether they agreed with it or not, Gia was now as much a part of it as we were. She knew things she shouldn't. Things that could destroy our family. Yet as I looked into her soft, rounded eyes, I trusted her.

Chapter Seventeen

Gia

The small recorder in my bra stabbed me in the chest every time I moved my arms, so I sat motionless and wordless as Enzo exchanged words with his crew.

"I'll see you next week, Bullseye. Let's meet at the smoke shop this time around," Enzo said as he pushed in the chair he'd been sitting in. "Can you guys take care of this?" He gestured toward Rudy's body. After a nod shared among the men, we exited through a one-way door with no handle on the outside at the back of the building.

I kept my arms crossed as the recorder slipped further into my bra, and I worried it would fall out. That would be a fatal mistake. I'd get the rough end of Enzo's business demeanor, and it wouldn't end well for me. We walked toward the car, and I sat in the passenger seat. I took a deep breath as the car rumbled toward the mansion. A nause-ating heaviness filled my chest from watching a man be murdered less than an hour ago. The Vigliones were involved in deeper shit than we ever imagined. Sex trafficking? Even if Enzo didn't see it as such, that was another level of federal charges. He scoffed at selling drugs but welcomed the sale of bodies?

"Why so quiet?" Enzo asked, shifting his glance between the road and me.

"Just didn't expect that," I said, as nonchalant as possible. We weren't an innocent family, and I wasn't in a place to pass judgment, but how could I not? I understood Rudy had to die—he couldn't let that kind of liability walk out the door—but to do it in such a bold way? I didn't expect that kind of recklessness from Enzo.

"I knew what was gonna happen, and I didn't want to bring you because of it," he said as his fingers gripped the steering wheel.

"Why did you?" I asked.

"If Silvio called that hit on you, I couldn't leave you there alone." His lips drew into a frown. I couldn't imagine not trusting my own father like that. If you didn't have family, what did you have?

"I can handle myself, especially if you gave me my damn gun back." I cocked a half smile at him.

"I don't trust you enough for that." He smirked at me and tipped my chin up with his finger.

I slapped his hand away. "Fuck you." He was right to lack trust in me, but it didn't make me any less mad.

• • •

Enzo

GIA'S HIPS swayed with every step as we strolled up the walkway toward the house. My eyes lingered on her incredible ass. She was a queen and she knew it. *I can't ever let her know what she does to me. Women like her get drunk off such power.*

"Will you wait up?" I yelled toward her as I quickened my steps to keep pace with her. She didn't slow down as she actively avoided my gaze. I grabbed her arm and spun her to face me.

"Enzo, I really have nothing to say to you." She stared at me with fire in her eyes. "I don't understand how you can trust me with your pistol and your dick, but not enough to let me have the only thing I can use to defend myself. You don't fucking trust me?" There was something about Gia that made me trust her with my life, but a larger part told me a girl like her would jerk your dick off with one hand while pulling a gun on you with the other.

"Gia . . ." My fingers pressed into the soft skin of her arm in a firm hold as the front door opened. She ripped her arm from me at the sight of Silvio staring at us.

Silvio eyed her up and down, his gaze hovering on the plunged neckline of her shirt. Gia covered her chest with crossed arms.

"Get in the house, now," Silvio demanded as he pointed toward the library. We walked inside, and Silvio's eyes darted back and forth between us. "Enzo!" He gestured toward the door, and I looked back at Gia. "She'll be fine, go!" he screamed, and it wasn't a choice any longer.

I stepped into her to hand her my keys, keeping one apart from the others as I offered them to her.

"Go to my room," I commanded her in a whisper. She grabbed the ring of keys, keeping her fingers on the one I'd been holding. I tried to tell her with my expression to go and lock the door. She nodded toward me, and the click of her heels disappeared.

Silvio slammed the door behind me as we walked into the library. He was so angry he was short of breath, anger squeezing his lungs. "What the fuck happened?" Silvio brushed a hand through his slick hair.

"Rudy . . ." I shook my head. "Motherfucker went to the goddamn feds."

"Did you even have proof?" Silvio paced the floor.

"I didn't need it. He confessed to all of us." I sat in the overstuffed leather chair.

"What exactly did he confess to?"

"Talking to the feds about sex trafficking from the—"

"Are you fucking kidding me?" Silvio groaned and dropped his shoulders. "And you decided it was a good idea to confront him in the goddamn club that's being investigated?"

"I had no—"

"And *that* is why a family like this could never be run by someone like you," Silvio hissed, jutting his finger at me.

"Oh, fuck off, Silvio." Heat rose to my face, filling my cheeks as anger bloomed in my chest and quickened my heart rate. "While you were stroking your ego in the Cayman fucking Islands, I had to handle business."

"And you handled business with that goddamn Silvani broad at your side?" Silvio slammed his fist on the table, and the glasses trembled from the force.

"You really wanna go there?" I stood and squared off to him. "I wouldn't have had to bring her along had you not sent your brother in after her! You take someone in on your word and you let her—" I couldn't even complete my sentence as anger ripped through my chest.

"Eh, she's a Silvani, son. She can handle a little roughin' up." A grotesque grin crept across Silvio's face.

"That's not the point! She's under my protection, so she's my responsibility."

"Yeah, I feel like that should probably change. She's making you lose your senses."

His words made my hand drop to my gun. Sweat slicked my fingers as they wrapped around the wooden grip.

"I bet she let you fuck her, didn't she?" Silvio's condescending words taunted me. "Tell me, son, how did she taste? Was it everything I imagined it would be?" He let out a groan as if he was fucking her in his mind.

"That ain't gonna happen." The threat rang clear in my unwavering voice. The thought of Silvio getting his hands on Gia made my stomach tighten. Even though he'd made me share with him in the past, no one else would touch Gia. *No one.* I'd make sure of that.

Silvio reached under his jacket and grasped his pistol. The difference between my pops and I was that I would hesitate before killing him. He looked down at my hip, at my hand clutching my gun.

"What are you gonna do, Enzo? Shoot me?" He chuckled. "You're going to risk this family? Our business? Everything we've worked for, all for some broad that gets your dick a little hard? You better start thinking with the right head."

"I am," I snarled as I unholstered my pistol and raised it toward Silvio.

His expression was emotionless, as if he were fully prepared to call my bluff. *Am I bluffing?* I cocked the hammer of the revolver and kept it trained on his thick neck. Silvio drew his pistol, the silver of it reflecting the light above us as he leveled the barrel on me. It was a Mexican standoff, an unwinnable fight.

The door swung open, and we both rerouted the barrels

to the doorway. Gia raised her hands, no emotion on her face despite the guns trained on her.

"What are you doing here?" Silvio demanded.

"I could hear the yelling, and I decided to jump in here before someone shot first. If you think the Silvanis haven't pulled guns on each other during heated discussions of family matters, you'd be mistaken." Gia lowered her hands, propping them on her hip. "Come on, put the guns down."

I looked at Silvio, back at Gia, and met my pop's gaze again. We relaxed a bit, staring at each other as we holstered our guns.

"This isn't over, Enzo," Silvio said with a harshness in his voice that made a chill crawl up my spine. Those same words spilled from Lorenzo's mouth.

"It never is," I said.

Chapter Eighteen

Gia

"We'll talk about this in my room." Enzo grabbed my arm and dragged me out of the library. I tried to plant my feet as he pulled me toward the stairs. He walked ahead of me, a noisy exhale wafting toward me from his lips. He motioned toward me. "Keys."

I handed the ring to him, and he fumbled with the individual keys as his frustration levels rose the closer he got to opening the door. My stomach tightened.

Enzo opened the door and motioned me inside. I hesitated for a moment before going into the room, wincing at the sound of the door slamming behind me.

"Are you out of your goddamn mind, Gia?" Enzo yelled.

"I probably shouldn't have intru—"

"No, Gia, you shouldn't have! You could have gotten yourself killed! Shit, it could have even been by my hand!" He gestured toward his gun and paced.

"I didn't think it would be a big deal," I said with a deflated drop in my shoulders. He was right, though. I should have known better than to get between him and his father.

"That whole situation in there makes me question how much I can protect you here," Enzo said as he brushed his hand through his hair. "Silvio has such a hard-on for you. It's not safe."

"If you'd just give me my—"

"No, Gia, goddamn it! You aren't getting your fucking gun! I think we should get you outta here." His jaw tensed.

The thought of going back home made my stomach and heart equally twist. I wanted to go back to my family and get away from these animals, but I didn't want to leave Enzo. Not yet. "I'm not going home."

Enzo met my gaze and walked toward me until our lips were nearly touching. "You have to."

The sadness in his words created an unexplainable draw toward his weakness, and I rose onto the tips of my toes, laced my hands around his neck, and kissed him. He allowed my advancement for a moment before he grabbed my hands and pushed me away.

"I'm not fucking doing this with you right now."

I dropped onto my heels and looked up at him, his words ripping through me and squeezing my stomach. "So . . . it was really just one night?" I asked, my words catching in my throat.

"That's what you wanted all along, right?" Enzo walked away from me and removed his shoes. He kicked them aside, unholstered his gun, and set it on the table beside him before walking to the bathroom with a blank expression on his face.

I stared at the gun as I slipped the shirt over my head, letting the recorder fall into my hand. I quickly shoved it into the front pocket of my bag. I changed into pajamas, my gaze still on the tempting weapon. *Why would he leave it? Is it a test? If I were him, it would have been a test.*

I crawled into bed, letting the blanket envelop me, lulling me with its warmth. Enzo came back from the bathroom, unbuckling his pants as he walked. He stripped off his dress pants and folded them before placing them on the dresser. His fingers worked the buttons off his dress shirt, frustration punctuating every motion. He tossed the dress shirt into a pile on the floor and collapsed onto the couch with a sigh.

As if he suddenly remembered the gun, he grabbed for it, looking at me as he did. His body only relaxed once he realized I never touched it, as much as I wanted to.

"Are you going to act like this all night?" I asked as I turned onto my back and looked up at the ceiling fan. Its chains rattled as it slowly turned.

"I ain't acting like nothing." He kicked his legs up, lay on the couch, and closed his eyes.

***

Enzo

THE TICKING of the clock on the table beside the bed grew louder and more noticeable than ever, and the sound of Gia or Atheist snoring drew my attention with every noisy suck of air. Every sound was amplified as my nerves ignited beneath my skin and sent a crawling sensation creeping across my flesh. I reached into the desk and pulled out a cigarette. Once I'd drawn the smoke into my lungs, I finally felt relief from the relentless anxiety that nagged at me. The hot smoke assaulted my lungs and left my body in a long exhale as I kept the cigarette dangling between my lips.

This is bad. I looked at Gia's shadowy form and rubbed my beard. *All of this is bad.* I sighed at the realization—my feelings were getting in the way of business. Making me careless. I didn't trust Gia as much as I wanted to. She was too involved in the game to be naïve enough for me. For this life. *What we did together? It has to be only one night.*

"Enzo?" Gia's voice was small, still heavy with sleep.

"Yeah, sorry I woke you. I just really needed a smoke," I said as I exhaled.

She peeled herself out of bed, a long t-shirt hanging to the middle of her thighs, and she walked to the couch with slow and sensual steps. I pulled my eyes away from her, only to feel her climb onto the couch with me. She forced me to scoot over to accommodate her, and I did with a heavy sigh. She nestled beside me, the smell of her shampoo mixing with the stale smell of smoke. I draped my arm over the back of the couch to avoid touching her.

"I wish you'd stop," she said with a yawn.

"Stop what?" I grabbed the cigarette out of my mouth and tapped the ash into a tray beside me.

"This." She gestured toward my arm.

"I'm not gonna fuck you again, Gia," I said with a harshness she deserved. She was relentless. Nothing worse than a Silvani with a bone.

"Not even if I beg?" She let her hand crawl to the front of my boxers, her fingers grazing me through them. I hardened at her touch almost immediately, like a goddamn junkie seeking that high again.

"No," I told her, this time with a fierier bite of the word as I grabbed her hand and moved it away from my lap.

She huffed and sat up. "Can I have a drag, at least?"

I handed her what was left of my cigarette, and she placed it between her full lips. I ached at the sight, imagining them on my cock. With a shake of my head, I pushed those thoughts aside. That would be easier had I never gotten a taste of being inside her.

"You seem quite shaken up from that discussion with Silvio," she said as she reached over me to flick the ash off the cigarette. The soft fullness of her chest grazed my dick. She was prying because she was a fucking Silvani at heart.

"I think I made a mistake going to the club to confront Rudy," I told her as I wiped my hand down my face.

"Why do you think that?"

"I shouldn't have shot him in the goddamn club. It could have been bugged." I grabbed the cigarette from her and took another hit as my nerves began to rub raw again. "I won't go to prison, Gia, even if they come for me."

"Nothing you can do now." She shrugged, as if she didn't understand the gravity of the situation. But she did. If anyone knew, it was her.

Several minutes of silence passed between us before I finally spoke. "Silvio thinks I'm unfit to run the family business. That I'm letting you get to my head." *Both of them.*

"When it's time for you to run the business, he won't have a choice, now, will he?" She handed the cigarette to me, and I squelched it in the tray. Smoke still rose from it, circling in the air. "You can run this shit however you want, but I hope you make better choices than he did."

"How do you mean?"

"He lets people involved with drugs into his circle, and he launders money through businesses that are dealing with sex trafficking. This is literally torn from the handbook of 'What Not to Do as a Crime Lord.'" She grinned with tight lips.

"We can't all be a perfect family like yours," I said. Everyone in her family would always think they were better than us.

Gia tapped her temple. "You don't have to be perfect, just smart."

"We're being led by the goddamn devil himself." I sighed. "And he will happily bring us all to hell with him."

Chapter Nineteen

Gia

The sun shining through the huge bay window woke me up. I was still snuggled against Enzo's side on the couch. I didn't remember falling asleep, but I remembered the hunger in my pelvis before I had. His chest rose and fell rhythmically, and I stared at him. He looked sweet. He looked innocent. Like he wasn't capable of all that he was. My hands trailed down his chest, hovering at his bare stomach. He was a thing of beauty, and I wanted him more than anything, maybe even more than my next breath at that moment. It was all I could think about.

My hand trembled as I reached over his lap and rubbed the front of his boxers. He hardened beneath my teasing touch, his head still in his hand as he slept. I peeled myself away from him and crawled to the floor. The carpet cushioned my knees as my fingers worked on the waistband of his boxers, trying to pull them down. Enzo grabbed my hand and stopped me with a smirk.

"I said no, babygirl." His eyes were still closed, lips

slightly open in a pout. He batted my hands away from his lap.

I sat up. "I want you." I grabbed his face, and he opened his eyes. They were a dark shade of blue I'd never seen before in another person. Enzo was as unique as those eyes. The ache in my pelvis intensified, wanting nothing more than to have him take me.

"Too bad," he said as he stroked my cheek. "I ain't giving you what you want." His smirk was devilish and teasing. A person like Enzo would use my desire against me.

"Come the fuck on," I whined.

"Girl, get off your knees." He dragged me onto the couch. "We have work to do today."

I would believe his restraint if he wasn't rock hard through his shorts. I drooled at the curves beneath the fabric. I wanted my mouth on him, but the more I showed him I wanted it, the harder he fought against it. Evil bastard.

"Fine." I threw my hands up in defeat and stood. He tried to ignore me as I squatted to dig through my bag for clothes. *Remember how much he hated the thought of me getting myself off?* My mind sadistically whispered. *Why not?*

I climbed back into his bed and lay on top of the comforter.

"Did you hear me when I said we have to go to work?" he asked.

"Yeah, yeah, I know," I said as I pulled my panties slowly down my thighs, tugging them to my ankles. They tumbled to the floor as I tossed them.

Enzo squinted his eyes at me. "What are you doing?" His voice was stern, and he sat up taller on the couch.

"If you aren't going to fuck me, I'm just going to play

with myself," I said with pouted lips as I spread my legs and let my fingers trail up my thighs.

Enzo stiffened his posture, a frown on his face. "Gia, stop," he said with a curl of his lip.

I let a soft moan roll off my tongue as I found the warm wetness between my legs.

"Gia!" he commanded, rising to his feet. He watched as my fingers glided along my skin, rubbing against my clit. I slipped my fingers inside the place I knew he wanted the most, even if he told me he didn't.

He was getting pissed about me touching myself. That pleasure was coming from my hand and my hand only. His cheeks flushed red with anger as he adjusted himself in his boxers. The pattern did nothing to hide every inch straining against his underwear. I stared at that V leading up from his pelvis and imagined tracing it with my tongue. My thoughts wandered to him talking down on me, making me feel as worthless as I sometimes felt. It was my guilty pleasure to feel emotional and physical pain, and his denial was definitely emotionally painful.

Enzo

I HATED SEEING her hands between her thighs, and it filled my gut with raw rage. She knew exactly what she was doing to me. I wanted to be the only thing making her come. *You can't fuck her,* I told myself as I watched her back arch. *She's making you weak.* I released a long breath, trying to calm the beast within me that wanted to tear her to shreds.

Gia's moans rolled over me and sent vibrations through

my spine. The sounds leaving her full lips drove me wild, but I couldn't show it. I ached for her, and she knew exactly what she was doing. Her eyes locked on mine as her hips moved, bucking against her fingers. *Jesus, Mary, and Joseph,* I groaned in the recesses of my mind.

I stepped toward her, her eyes following me. With a firm grasp, I yanked her hand from between her legs and halted her movement. She gasped, as if she were fucking surprised.

"I said to stop, Gia," I commanded. That close to her, my gaze fell on the soft, dark hairs between her legs, and I smelled the light aroma of her excitement. My cock throbbed as every fucking inch of her overwhelmed my senses. "Are you really playing dirty like this? You don't think I fucking want that?" I gestured toward the warmth between her legs.

"Take it, then," she whispered before biting her lip.

Fuck, I thought as I leaned over her, my lips hovering above hers. She reached up and kissed me, drawing my face toward her. I melted into her touch for only a moment and pushed my hand between her legs, rubbing and growling at the wetness against my skin. She moaned against my mouth as if my touch electrified her.

With my fingers inside her, the thought of Silvio pried into my mind. He thought so little of my ability to run this family. But he was right. Gia made me forget my responsibilities, having needed to be at the club thirty fucking minutes ago.

I can't do this. I shook my head and pulled my hand away from her.

"Get dressed," I said sternly, leaving her on the bed as I went into the bathroom. "We have to go to work."

By the time I got dressed, she'd finally put on some

clothes. I wasn't even sure if she finished herself off. I refused to wait around to see. I pushed the ends of my purple dress shirt into my black pants. My gaze roved over Gia's curves, enamored by the way her pants hugged the cuffs of her ass.

She walked behind me, quietly, clearly seething.

She doesn't understand. She doesn't have to worry about being the boss of shit, not while her brother is still alive. All she has to worry about is defending herself and her family name.

Chapter Twenty

Gia

The drive in the car was suffocatingly silent. He turned the music on, and I quickly flicked it off and leaned back in my seat with my arms crossed. Petty? Yes. But I wanted him to hear the insufferable silence with me.

"Goddamn it, Gia, what's your problem?" he snapped, but I didn't respond, didn't even acknowledge that he'd spoken at all. "Fuck you, too," he said as he gripped the wheel harder.

In his frustration, he nearly passed the turn toward the club. With a quick tug of the wheel, he took a fast turn, making my stomach lurch into my chest. He pulled into the parking lot and exhaled before climbing out of the car.

"Are you coming in?" he asked as he bent down and looked at me still sitting in the passenger seat, twirling my hair.

"Yeah, give me a minute." I took out a cigarette and lit it. Smoke billowed from the open window beside me.

He looked at his watch, an obnoxious gesture that made

my lip curl. "Gia, we have to go. We're late. Come on!" he commanded.

I rolled my eyes at him and extinguished the cigarette in the console between the seats. "Fine, you don't have to yell." I climbed out of the car and slammed the door.

We started toward the club entrance, walking beneath the faded awning leading to the sidewalk. The club was one I recognized, but not when it was closed. There was no music reverberating inside your chest and no bodies pressed together, and the interior smelled stale instead of like sweat and sex. Enzo's steps echoed on the linoleum dance floor, and the bar stools creaked as the men lining the bar turned toward him. They looked at me, sizing me up. I flashed a quick nod toward Bullseye and Kenny. I didn't recognize the rest of them.

"Enzo." Bullseye stood and greeted him. They shook hands, and Enzo sat beside him.

One of the suited men went behind the bar to grab Enzo a drink. He looked at me. "Do you want a drink, Silvani?" Despite his nice gesture, he looked at me with mistrust.

"I'll take a glass of bourbon, please." I sat beside Kenny. "Do I know you?" I asked the other man as he placed my drink in front of me.

"I know you and your family. You don't need to know me." He tightened his lips as he went toward his seat in front of the bar.

Enzo pulled the men into conversation as they flocked around him. I hardly heard the intentionally hushed words between them.

"Kenny Agostino, right?" I gestured to the man beside me as I brought the glass toward my lips and let it hover there.

He glanced at me before he steered his gaze away. I took a sip of my drink, the cool liquid burning my throat with its strength. I pulled out a cigarette and lit it, holding it between my fingers. Kenny watched me from the corner of his dark eye and fidgeted with his leg.

I leaned into him, my chest accentuated. "Why are you so afraid to look at me?"

He cleared his throat nervously. "Because you're Enzo's girl."

I leaned into him with a pout of my lips. "I am not anyone's girl," I whispered in his ear, getting a waft of cologne as he brushed his dark hair back.

Enzo's gaze met mine. Seeing my close proximity to his colleague, his eyes squinted as I leaned away from Kenny.

"I'll be right back." Enzo got up and led the other men into a back room.

Kenny tapped his fingers on the bar, desperate to avoid my gaze.

My fingers explored his thick brown hair as I pulled him toward me. He tried to pull away from my kiss for a moment before giving in and letting it happen. I crawled onto his lap as our kiss intensified. It was enough to make me ache, but I was aching for Enzo.

Enzo

My fingers grazed my chest pocket. "Shit, I forgot my cigarettes at the bar."

The moment I opened the door, I saw the worst thing I'd ever seen, and I'd seen some shit. Mangled bodies, raped wives, and decapitated fucking children. What I was seeing now was Gia on Kenny's lap, kissing him. Kenny's hands remained at his sides. Anger raced through my veins. I could only hear the sound of my heartbeat as I unholstered my revolver. I walked behind them and cocked it at the back of Kenny's head. Gia jumped between me and Kenny, wiping the lipstick off her face.

"Move, Gia," I demanded.

"No, don't. Kenny had nothing to do with it," she said as she reached for the barrel of the revolver. Stupid girl. "I was just trying to make you jealous," her voice was flat and even, as if she didn't just slap a target on poor Kenny's back. Not that she'd care if she did. Gia only thought about what she wanted.

Kenny turned around and stared at me, emotionless. "Your girl is thirsty, Enzo. That's not my problem."

This motherfucker.

Gia flinched at Kenny's taunting words, knowing that such a statement probably deserved a bullet. I narrowed my eyes and grabbed her roughly by the arm. The other men came out of the back room and tensed.

"What's going on?" Bullseye asked, gesturing toward my drawn gun.

"Nothing," I snarled. "I just have some business to handle." I looked at Kenny. "This ain't over." *Nothing is ever fucking over.* I holstered my gun again and dragged her toward the back door. My fingers dug into her skin so hard she whined as she tried to keep up with me.

We stepped into the humid air. The door slammed behind us, causing Gia to flinch. I pushed her against the concrete wall, scraping her skin. I was too angry to care. My hand shot up to an area of the wall beside her head, and my other hand hovered on the butt of my revolver.

"Are you out of your goddamn mind?" I was fucking livid. She fucked up a step too far that time.

"I . . ." she started to explain, but it just made me angrier.

"Do I have to go in there and kill one of my fucking friends? My *friend*, Gia! You know how hard it is to have friends in this business." *He wasn't no friend, though. You don't put your hands on another man's woman. Especially mine.*

"I told him we weren't together. It's not his fault," she said with a drop of her shoulders. "Which we really aren't. If I was yours, maybe you'd actually fuck me." She rolled her eyes and avoided my gaze.

I slapped the wall beside her head, fury rising until it almost choked off my breath. "You really did this because I didn't fuck you? Are you kidding me?" Her childish antics disgusted me. It was life or death in this lifestyle, yet she thought it was a game.

My hands moved on autopilot as I unholstered my gun and drew it on her. I pressed the cool metal against her face, brushing the hair off her cheek. She looked up at me, her face utterly calm. It pissed me right the fuck off. *It ain't normal for a bitch to act so strange with a loaded gun to her head.*

I narrowed my eyes as I plunged my hand down the front of her pants, and she gasped at my touch. She was soaked.

"You like this shit, don't ya?" I tightened my lips.

I thought I knew Gia, but maybe I didn't. I lowered the barrel, trailing the metal along the front of her pants, jutting it between her legs. I raised it, rubbing it along her as she grinded against it. When I pulled it away from her, her hips followed forward, begging for more. I turned her around, her breath now rolling over the cracks in the concrete, and pressed her into the wall with my body. The barrel of my gun made her shiver as I eased it down her back. My finger remained off the trigger. I had no intention of hurting Gia, even if she deserved it.

My fingers worked open my buckle as my revolver rested along the small of her back. The sound of my zipper falling was the only interruption to the silence. She pressed her hips against me.

"Is this what you fucking want?" I tugged her pants down, not caring if I ripped the soft fabric. She wasn't wearing panties. "Was this your plan all along?" I asked with the roughness she craved. I was fucking pissed she'd stooped so low, but it also kind of turned me on. Her desperation was sexy. Which was fucked. "You wanted to be a whore? Huh?"

She flashed her eyes back at me, nodding for only a moment before I pressed her face into the wall. I pulled out my cock and rubbed it between her legs. Her pussy coated me, and I throbbed as I rubbed myself against her clit.

"You're a goddamn bitch, you know that? Only thinking about your fucking self. About getting your pussy filled. I ain't even that bad, and I've wanted you to wet my dick for fucking *years*."

She whimpered in agreement. She knew what she'd done, and there was no guilt in her as she grinded against my dick.

I holstered my revolver and used both hands to grab her waist. She leaned against the wall, raising her hips. I surged within her and stretched her pussy, somehow even more than last time. I thrust against her smooth ass, which fit so perfectly against my pelvis. She felt incredible, like something I could only dream of. I fucked her hard, just like she wanted, as if she were a whore. I fisted her hair and pulled her toward me. My hand wrapped around her throat, squeezing as I pushed into her and held my position as deep as I could go, giving her no choice but to take every fucking inch of me within her. The noises leaving her mouth were born of pain mixed with pleasure.

"Tell me what I am, Enzo," she whispered.

"You're a goddamn whore, and I can't even trust you alone for five minutes."

She melted into me, as if my words were Xanax. I grabbed her chin and craned her neck. Then the gravity of what she'd done hit me.

She made a mockery of me in front of my men. "You don't deserve any more of this," I said as I pulled away. Her body pressed against me, begging me to stay within her. *We ain't playing this game.* I unholstered my gun, fisted her hair, and held the barrel up to her pretty face. I cocked it, and the metallic click made her tremble. "If you ever touch one of my friends again, you're both dead. Do you understand?"

Her face relaxed, as if she was in heaven and the devil couldn't touch her. But she was in hell, and I would rip her the fuck apart if I had to.

Chapter Twenty-One

Gia

We drove back toward his house in silence. My mind wasn't silent, though. It raced with thoughts. There was an aching throb between my legs and an uncomfortable slickness between my thighs. Having a taste of him was worse than if he'd avoided fucking me altogether. The feel of his gun against my cheek and down the sensitive skin of my back . . . *oh god*. His anger made me weak and allowed me to be something other than strong for a few minutes. I wasn't worried about being the boss of shit. I was only the feeble girl everyone else got to be.

I twirled my hair around my finger as I tightened my lips. What I had done was wrong. Very wrong. I didn't mean to bring Kenny into mine and Enzo's game. For a sick second, he seemed like a worthy casualty of war.

"Enzo," I began.

He ignored me, keeping his hands tight on the steering wheel. His cheeks pulsed, which only happened when he was beyond angry.

"Can we please talk about it?" I asked.

His eyes flashed to me for only a moment before jumping back to what was ahead of us—the sun as it teased the horizon and began to disappear.

When we pulled into the garage, he parked and put his elbow on the padding beneath the window beside him. His fingers traced his lips, as if he were trying to figure out what to do with me. His eyes darted and his left leg shook. He climbed out of the car and shut the door without acknowledging me as he walked away. I hurried to catch up with him, my heels clanking on the concrete with each uneven step.

"Enzo?" a gruff voice called from the library the moment we walked in. I avoided Silvio's gaze as he motioned toward Enzo. He didn't look back at me as he followed his father behind the two large wooden doors.

I headed toward the bedroom, taking my time to observe the family photos along the halls. Enzo had mastered a resting bitch face. He never looked happy. Silvio always displayed a wide grin, his fat cheeks hiding the sides of his smile. His arms draped around his two younger sons, who were also smiling. Silvio treated Enzo like the black sheep.

The light illuminated the room as I flipped the switch, and Atheist raced toward me the moment I walked in. His large body crashed into my knees as he slammed into me, and I squatted and rubbed his head between my hands. As I stood and gripped the waistband of my pants to change, the door swung open.

❦

Enzo

THE SIGHT OF GIA—HER hands grasping her pants, the fabric halfway off her bare skin—was too much for me. Her stunt got back to Silvio, which didn't help my cause. How could I run a family business when I couldn't even keep Gia under control? I never expected her to stoop so low to get what she wanted. But I kind of also did.

Her hands hovered at the bones protruding from her hips. She looked at me with lips drawn into a frown.

I stepped forward, fisting her hair and yanking her toward me as she squealed against my grasp. "You made me look like a fool in front of my men," I hissed.

Her eyes rounded, not with fear, but a melting excitement. *Goddamn it, Gia.* She reached toward the front of my pants and groped at my unintentional hardness.

"No, Gia," I commanded, batting her hand away from me.

"I'm sorry," she whispered, pouting her lips.

"You aren't sorry. This is exactly what you fucking wanted." My eyes locked on the soft curves of her lips. Heat rose from my groin and moved toward my stomach. I wanted to punish her, but there was no punishing Giovanna Silvani. Punishing her only punished me, and I was fucking over it. She'd take a mouthful of me, and I wasn't going to be kind about it. "Get down on your goddamn knees," I said as I used my free hand to work my pants down.

Her eyes grew wide, her lip quivering. She hesitated for a moment before letting herself drop to the floor.

"You can't be trusted, Giovanna." I used her hair to bring her mouth toward my cock. I slapped the side of her face, and her cheek reddened. "Suck me and show me how sorry you are."

She looked up at me with doe eyes as I shoved my dick past her loose lips. There was no resistance as I slammed into the back of her throat. She could no doubt taste herself, the remnants of her pussy still coating me. She gagged, gasping for air as I thrust my hips forward. My hand gripped her hair in an unwavering grasp. I refused to let her off my dick. She struggled for breath as I stretched her throat. Both her cheeks reddened as her body begged for more air. I pulled her head away from me, a trail of spit clinging to me from her lower lip. Tears fell down her cheeks, but they weren't from sadness.

She sat back on her heels and looked up at me as she wiped the drool from her mouth. Nothing. Absolutely nothing from her. No residual fear or discomfort. She was fucking insatiable. I was entirely unsure if she even had a heart in her chest. Did she feel *anything* at all?

"Stand up and get undressed," I snapped.

I felt annoyed with her, even as she sent pleasurable shivers up my spine. I let my pants fall to the ground and stepped out of them, along with my shoes. My fingers worked the buttons of my dress shirt down, letting the fabric spread and expose my stomach, tense with frustration. As she watched me sit on the bed, she slipped her pants down, exposing the tanned skin between her legs that I *needed* to feel again. There was no other option at this point. She lifted her shirt above her head and dropped it to the ground. Her fingers clasped her bra straps as she slid them off her shoulder, then unclipped it behind her back.

Gia remained wordless as she stepped toward me and crawled onto my lap. She encased my thighs with her own. She sat back, hovering over my length, letting herself rest over the burning heat of my cock. My hands raced over her sides and toward her chest. She winced as I grabbed her roughly, toying with her nipples between my fingers. She rocked her hips, gliding over me and leaving a wet mess.

"You're disgusting," I whispered as I used her hair to pull her face toward mine.

"How disgusting?" She reached down to put me inside her and gasped as she lowered herself onto me, nearly reaching my pelvis.

I sank into her warm, inviting pussy and dropped my head back with a groan. "I shouldn't even be giving you my cock after your *pathetic* and *desperate* attempt at getting it. You're worse than a fucking dog. At least they're faithful." My words bit, tearing into her, but they didn't make her moan.

With every insult I hurled at her, she grinded her hips harder and faster against me. It was a goddamn work of art the way she arched her back and grabbed a fistful of her own hair as she rode me. Her lips parted to allow the moans to escape freely from them. She tensed around me, her body growing rigid and her movements growing uneven. I grabbed her and pulled her chest against mine, a hand firmly on her hip. She couldn't even rock her hips because of how tightly I pressed her against my body. She released a frustrated groan as I throbbed within her. She looked up at me, her cheeks flushed.

"Please let me come," she begged.

"Not yet, babygirl." I pulled out of her, and she sighed. I flipped her onto her back, crawling between her legs. My fingers grazed the soft flesh of her thighs as her hips bucked with desire. "You don't get to come until I say so," I groaned against her neck as I kissed her. Once her breaths became more even, I surged within her and let her warmth surround me once more. I fought back my ultimate pleasure, the nagging feeling burning in my pelvis, because I didn't want her to come until she was suffering.

My thrusts were rough but even, and every buck of my hips made her tremble. My lips fell to her perfect breasts, flicking her nipples with a hungry tongue. Her legs wrapped around me, pulling me into her. She moved beneath me, grinding against my pelvis, her moans rolling over mine. She tightened around me again, and I knew she was getting close. I pulled out of her just as she began to spasm—the very tail end of edging her. Her frustrated growl was animalistic, as if coming had morphed into a need and instead of a mere desire. I stroked my cock against her and understood her pain. My dick was getting pissed with me, and I needed to spill every ounce of my stress and frustration into her.

"Please, Enzo. I can't . . ." She couldn't even finish her sentence, her desperation overcoming her.

Her hand lowered to rub herself, trying to get the relief she needed, but I grabbed it just before it reached her clit and pinned both wrists above her head. I smirked at her, biting into my lower lip as I drove my hips back inside her. My weight covered her, pinning her as I grinded my pelvis against her clit. She tensed again, her chest lurching upward as her back arched. She squeezed the fuck out of my cock. She looked at me as if she expected me to stop, and I *wanted* to. But the fire in my pelvis rushed through my cock and I *had* to come.

"Come for me, Giovanna." I whispered her name in her ear, low and gravelly. Exactly how she liked it. She came, her body shuddering against me.

Goddamn it, Gia.

Chapter Twenty-Two

Gia

I tried to tune out the arguing by dropping my face into my palm.

Enzo tensed and sat taller, gesturing with his hands. "I told you time and time again, Bullseye, we don't fuck with guns. Not the sale or the transportation. Do we really want to add the ATF to the list of federal agencies on our asses?"

Bullseye shrugged, pulling a cigar from his lips. "It's a good payout, boss. I think it would be worth the risk."

Enzo wiped at his face, shaking his head. "I said no."

Bullseye tightened his mouth. "What if I told you I already scored a deal on a case of rifles?"

Enzo rubbed his temples. "Please tell me you didn't."

"Just one, and it's a huge sum of money. It's an easy transfer across a few state lines," Bullseye said with a shrug.

"Just a few state lines. Yeah, easy," Enzo said, his voice laced with sarcasm.

Kenny caught my gaze for a moment before quickly dropping his. At least he was alive.

While they argued, Enzo's hand dropped to my bare thigh beneath the large wooden table. My skirt had risen when I sat on the cozy chair in the back area of the club. His fingers gripped at the soft skin of my inner thigh anytime he raised his voice, pushing that frustration into my flesh. His fingers climbed up my thighs, raking my skin with his nails. A shiver radiated down my spine and crept toward my pelvis. I looked around at the men in the room, several I'd met and others that still eyed me because I was a Silvani. They didn't seem to notice Enzo's crawling hand, or if they did, they didn't dare say anything.

"Ah, fuck! What a pass!" Bullseye yelled and clapped his hands.

Everyone turned their attention to the football game playing on the large television. Enzo took the opportunity to slide his warm hand against me. My lips parted as a silent gasp rolled off my tongue and past my lips. There were no panties between me and his strong hand. The heat radiated off his skin as he curled his finger, rubbing my clit. His upper arm remained mostly still as he circled me with his fingertip. I dropped my head into my hands, covering my mouth with them.

Bullseye turned to face Enzo, and my body tensed. He didn't look at me while pleasure began a slow burn between my legs. I felt the crawling rise of heat from my chest, mottling my cheeks. I looked fucking guilty. I shook one leg nervously. With a sideways glance, I tried to tell him to stop. When he didn't, I uncovered my mouth for a moment and mouthed the word at him. He bit into his lower lip, living for my discomfort. Instead of stopping, his touch grew rougher.

I couldn't hear any of the words around me. I only felt Enzo tense when he raised his voice and extended that frustration through his fingertips into me. The growing wetness between my legs began to make noise, and I tried to tighten my thighs to slow his movement. He pinched the inside of my thigh, making me spread my legs with a jolt. The more the sound of excitement gathered as he rubbed me, the harder he bit into his lip. Did he want them to hear how fucking wet he made me? Or maybe he just didn't give a damn if they did.

My hips subtly rocked as a ball of pleasure balanced between my legs. I couldn't drop it. He sank a finger into me, and a noise escaped my slack lips. I cleared my throat out of panic and looked around the room to see if anyone had heard. No one was paying attention, but Enzo had a shit-eating grin all over his stupid face.

He loves to fuck with me.

I looked down at his lap and could see how hard he was, the angles of his dress pants showcasing his excitement. With his other hand, he adjusted himself before diving into another conversation about agencies and gu—

Oh god.

I nearly dropped the ball from between my legs. A sudden creeping sensation spread through my hips and into my pelvis, landing at his fingertips. I trembled, trying to control my legs, to maintain my composure as my abdomen tightened, tilting my pelvis up. *Please stop.* I closed my eyes and bit down on my lip, stifling my moans.

"Are you alright, Gia?" Bullseye asked with a rise in his eyebrow.

His words made me jump and pushed me away from the edge for a moment. "I'm fine, just, look at that pass . . ." I allowed my eyes to dart back to the TV, unsure if anyone even made a pass at all.

The boys erupted in laughter and applauded for a

moment before turning back to each other for business. It was all background noise. My focus was on the unbearable sensation growing between my legs.

I rocked against him, my movements guiding me toward the edge, almost dropping and shattering that ball of pleasure that I kept clenched between my thighs. They quivered and with an arch of my back, I nearly came. It was all too much. When my body couldn't stop spasming and I felt out of control, I pushed the chair back. It scraped against the floor with a distracting sound, and I withdrew from his touch. Everyone looked at me.

"I'll be right back," I said as I stood and tugged my skirt down.

"Are you okay?" Bullseye asked.

My face twisted, and I threw a quick nod his way before running toward the bathroom. Every step electrified me, the sensations so damn strong that the smallest amount of friction felt like a whole hand. I let the bathroom door close behind me and pressed myself against it. I felt like I couldn't catch my breath, as if it was all stuck in my gut, buried where my orgasm lay.

The door whipped open, startling me as it knocked into me. Enzo walked into the bathroom and smiled.

"What?" I snapped.

"Just wanted to make sure you weren't doing something you shouldn't be." He pressed his body against me. "Or touching anything you shouldn't be." His words rolled off his tongue and fucked my ears.

Goddamn it.

He sounded real fucking Italian at that moment, like the sadistic boss he'd probably wind up being one day.

"What the fuck is wrong with you?" I hissed, shifting my weight from one leg to another.

"What? This?" He licked his fingers, tasting me on them. He rubbed his thumb along my lip with a grin on his face.

He jerked my skirt up and put his hand between my legs. I gasped. His touch nearly began where it left off, the sensations too strong to control. Enzo pushed his fingers inside me and rocked them as I shuddered against his chest. I needed to come. My body was a ticking time bomb, his fingers the fuse, and I was ready to explode. He slammed his fingers inside me until I gripped his arms so hard I thought I might rip his shirt. I bit my lip until I tasted blood.

"Is this why you didn't wear panties? Huh? So I could finger fuck you like this?"

Of course that wasn't the reason. But maybe a part of me hoped he would.

"Please," I pleaded. I looked up at him, afraid he would stop me, halt it like he loved to do.

He didn't.

I came in a gush of pleasure. The ball dropped and shattered between my legs. He shook his hand off, wearing a grin that would make the devil blush. He brought his fingers to my lips and slipped them into my mouth. I wanted to drop to my knees right there and replace his fingers with what I really wanted. He fisted my hair and kissed me.

"You'll owe me later," he said playfully as he bit my lower lip.

I sure fucking will. I melted into the wall and tugged down my skirt. It clung to my skin, and the fabric where I'd been sitting was cold and damp from my excitement.

He looked back at me once more before closing the bathroom door and leaving me awash in bliss.

Goddamn it, Enzo.

Chapter Twenty-Three

Enzo

I woke up to Gia snoring softly in my arms. It was still dark outside. She looked angelic, with the moon silhouetting her features, but we both knew she was no angel. I wanted to make her repay the favor from last night, but I was too worked up, even for her.

Atheist whined beside the bed.

"You have to go out, boy?" I asked with a pat on his head as I slid from beneath her.

"Where you going?" she asked with a yawn.

"To let Atheist out." I slid my feet into slippers and reached for the doorknob.

"Wait, I'll come," she said as she sat up and wiped her eyes, still heavy with sleep.

Gia slipped on flip-flops, and I opened the door to the balcony. Atheist took the stairs at a racing pace as he cut us off. He danced at the bottom, the barred fence preventing him from going into the yard to feel the grass beneath his paws.

I opened the gate, and it rattled and scraped against the concrete pavers lining the small landing as Atheist pushed at it. He nearly took out my knees as he ran toward the grass and disappeared into the yard, past where the floodlights illuminated the dark grounds. The silence was broken again as I heard three sounds that made my heart sink: Atheist barking, a silenced pistol shot, and then a pained yelp.

My feet moved before I could even process the act. The most rational action would have been to grab my revolver from the bedroom, but the thought of losing Atheist over-powered every other sense. *What kind of piece of shit goes for a man's dog?* Gia ran after me as I raced through the trees, looking around despite the blackness that veiled every side of me. I listened for the sound of his collar; his tags always clanged together with every step he took. There was a disgusting silence around me. *If someone killed my damn dog, I will find them and turn them inside fucking out.*

The sound of another silenced shot rang out, followed by the familiar sound of a bullet whizzing past me. I looked back at Gia and dived into her, knocking her to the ground and covering her with my body. Several more shots rang out, and I felt utterly helpless. I'd never felt like that before, like the world around me was fucking breaking.

Gia lifted her hip, raised her arm, and fired two shots into the air. The shots weren't silenced in the slightest, and it left my ears ringing. I shook out my jaw, rubbing the area in front of my ears. All gunfire ceased, and my mouth dropped open. She was holding her pocket pistol, the one I'd hidden from her.

"Gia!" I ran my hand up her arm until I felt the cool metal and snatched it from her grasp. "Where the hell did you even hide this?" I couldn't figure out where she'd been carrying or when the fuck she'd even gotten her gun.

Just as she was about to respond, a soft whimpering came from the direction of the house. Atheist limped toward the area lit by the floodlights. I got to my feet, biting the inside of my cheeks as I ran for my dog, nearly losing my slippers as they slid off the backs of my feet. *Not Atheist, pretty much anyone besides him.* Atheist was my best friend when I had no one. *That goddamn dog loves me no matter how shitty of a person I am.*

As I wrapped him up in my arms, I saw a bleeding wound in his armpit. Thick red blood poured from it. He whimpered but continued to wag his nub of a tail at me. Family? Nah, gain the trust of a dog and you'll see real loyalty.

I tossed Gia's pistol to her. "Go back upstairs. Lock the door. Don't open it for no one."

❖

Gia

I caught my pistol in midair and pocketed it in the waistband of my shorts. With a grunt, Enzo lifted Atheist. The dog whined against his touch. He nodded toward the gate, and I opened it to let him carry Atheist toward the garage. I locked it behind him and ran up the stairs to the room. My heart was still racing as I closed the balcony door and locked it.

I was finally alone in the bedroom. I reached into my bag, rustled around, and pulled out the little recorder. It balanced perfectly on the curve of my open palm. The holes in the little square box were tiny, but big enough to absorb every word since I'd been there. I closed it in my fist, torn between the truth and the abnormal beat of my heart at the thought of Enzo.

I walked into the bathroom and looked at myself in the mirror. My hair was tossed into a bun on my head, dried leaves sticking to it. *Enzo dived on top of me when the gunshots rang out.* My shoulders fell forward at the weight of betraying my family. I had one fucking job to do. I clutched the recorder to my chest as the battle inside me raged on.

I tossed the recorder down, and it broke into pieces as it skittered across the tile floors. I picked up the remnants and put it back into my bag, tucked away. The pistol rubbed against my skin, reminding me of its presence. I pulled it out and turned the safety on. I didn't know what made me grab it or why I felt the urge to follow Enzo. He'd let Atheist out a million times since I'd been there, and I usually didn't join him. Regardless, I was glad I had, even though I was positive I'd hear all about it from Enzo later.

The bed welcomed my tired body into it, and I curled up and wrapped myself in the weighted blanket. I struggled with anxiety. I knew how much that dog meant to Enzo. Atheist was the one thing in the world Enzo could be weak around. I couldn't sleep, no matter how hard I tried, and all I could do was wait. Waiting was worse than knowing.

THE DOOR CLOSED, and I craned my head to look at the clock. He'd returned without Atheist after being gone for hours, which made my heart drop somewhere below my diaphragm. I sat up, studying his face for clues.

"Atheist?" I asked. His expressionless features were too hard to read.

"They're keeping him overnight. They think he'll be okay." Enzo sat on the bed with a sigh and rubbed his temples. He dropped his gaze and his eyes widened as he pulled the fabric of his shirt away from him to examine it. With a snarl, he tore it off and ripped it to shreds. "Fuck!" he yelled as he dropped his head into his hands. "I can't lose him, Gia."

I scooted toward him, but he shrugged out of my grasp, lifting his hand toward me. I recoiled. He looked at me with a slack jaw and wide eyes before lowering his hand and bringing it toward my cheek. He pulled me against his chest and just held me. My posture remained rigid within his embrace.

"Who do you think it was?" I rubbed his thigh, trying to comfort the nervous motions of his leg.

"Who the fuck knows, Gia. It could have been anyone. We have quite a few enemies." His gaze shot up and stared at the pistol on the nightstand. His lips formed a tight line. "I hope you didn't think I'd forget that little stunt. How long have you had your gun?"

"I found it a few days ago."

"And you weren't gonna tell me?" He grabbed a fistful of my hair and craned my neck to force me to look at him.

"There's nothing to tell. It's my gun."

"You ain't gonna walk around my house with a goddamn gun."

"Why? Because you don't trust me? Shit, Enzo, if I wanted to kill you, I would have done it *days ago*!" I rolled my eyes at him, and he jerked me by my hair.

His frustration boiled over like rolling waves of hot

water, and he threw me face down on the bed. His hands hooked my shorts as he jerked them down my thighs.

"Enzo, stop," I commanded, my voice wavering. Despite my verbal protest, my body ached for him.

"Fuck you, Gia," he growled. He tugged down his sweatpants, and his cock dropped between my legs from behind me, rubbing against my inner thigh. "I'm gonna take what's mine," he said through clenched teeth as he grabbed my hips.

"Enzo . . ." I pleaded, though my hips rose to meet his.

He thrust into me, making me gasp as he surged within me. He didn't care if I wanted it or not. He only cared that it was what *he* wanted. I was his to take. *And I fucking want him to take it.* He pounded against the soft curves of my ass, filling the air with a sound that made me weak. I melted into the mattress.

"I told you, you owe me," he said as he fisted my hair and drew me toward him. He wrapped his arm around the front of my body, snaking it up my shirt to grab hold of my chest. His animalistic growls rolled over my neck, making me shiver. "You're fucking mine, do you understand me?" he said through clenched teeth as he fucked me.

I whimpered against his roughness, and it just made him drive his hips harder. He was using all his strength, his muscles tense in his arms as he kept me pinned against him. I felt the entirety of the power inside Enzo Viglione.

The pressure was too much at this angle. Even an inch of him was pushing me too far. I tried to lean forward, but he held his grasp, slamming into me with a callousness that I equally hated and loved. The pain inside me lit a burning wildfire within my pelvis that traveled up my spine and crawled inside my brain. I thought only of the pain he poured into me and the pleasure it gave him. It made my body tingle, and a shiver rode downward like a tidal wave.

"Enzo, I can't take any more," I begged. I worried he would tear me in half, and I was only half okay with that.

"You have to," he growled against my cheek before trailing down to bite my neck. His thrusts slowed and grew more ragged, and I welcomed the release of tension inside me. He groaned as he thrust one more time with a final deep drive of his hips. He throbbed inside me.

He pulled away from me, letting his hand drop from my chest. I toppled against the bed, still half naked and covered in sweat. I rolled onto my back, staring at him as his hard eyes softened. He grabbed me roughly and pulled me into him, hugging me. He brushed the hair from my face, wiping away tears that had silently and unknowingly fallen down my cheeks.

"I'm sorry," he whispered, his shoulders dropping. "After everything—"

"Enzo, I wanted it." I looked up at him, biting my lip.

"I hurt you, though." He let his fingers walk along my skin, from my stomach to between my legs, and put his hand against my pussy, coated with the mess of our excitement. I melted into his touch and drew his hand toward my mouth, licking his fingers, tasting the both of us on them. He growled as he pulled me into him and kissed me. "I was just so goddamn frustrated. You have no idea what you do to me, Gia."

I do know, because you do the same fucking thing to me.

Chapter Twenty-Four

Enzo

The sun rose, assaulting my eyes behind my lids as it shone through the huge bay windows. Who the fuck put a big ass window like that facing the path of the sun every damn morning? I turned over and groaned as I reached for the curtains and slammed them shut. My naked body reminded me of last night, and her naked body beside me flooded me with memories of her. I'd selfishly taken her perfect body and used it for my most primal desire. I relieved the stress ripping through me by ripping into her.

My eyes moved down her body. Her skin was soft and smooth, flawless except for some random scars from this life. I ran my finger down her thigh, stopping at a scar that looked like it may have been from a bullet. She groaned softly and turned over. The sight of the curves of her full ass, with hips to grab onto, made me hard all over again. It was a constant cycle around her. During the most mundane moments, when my body finally relaxed, I'd catch a glimpse of her and get hard. Sometimes it was nothing more than her annoyed sighs, the sound of them enough to make me throb. *Do I dare let her into my heart? Bring her into the dark places in my mind?*

I shook my head.

"What are you staring at?" she grumbled as she turned to face me.

"Nothing," I said with no emotion, even though it raced through my veins.

Gia wiped her eyes, trying to rid herself of sleep.

The door down the hall opened and shut, and Gia white-knuckled the sheet over her chest. I heard the familiar rustle of the tags, and I pretty much leapt out of bed.

"Atheist?" I called to him. I looked at a text on my phone.

Sammy: *Picked up the beast.*

He wasn't doing it for me, or even Atheist. That sly dog went and picked him up first thing this morning because he looked for any reason to go to the vet's office and hit on the secretary there. The whole office was on our books, so he didn't need to pick up my damn dog to pay her a visit. They'd stitched up enough of us, furred or otherwise.

Atheist limped into the room, and I dropped to my knees to rub his head. My heart felt real fucking full for a moment. The white bandage stood out against his jet-black coat. Atheist limped to Gia and put his head on the bed with a long whine.

"Boy, I know, but you can't jump up here," she said as she sat up and petted him. "This dog is more than just a dog to you, huh?"

"Of course. He's family." My gaze dropped unintentionally, drawing Gia's astute attention.

"There's more to this than what you told me, isn't there?"

"Nah. There's nothing more to talk about." I shook my head, locking my heart with a steel chain.

How could I tell Gia about the abuse I faced without her seeing me differently afterward? It wasn't just Silvio's perverted fantasies, but it was abuse at the hands of "family." People my pops welcomed into our lives and home. Atheist wasn't alive during the abuse, but he was with me at the worst time in my life—when my mother died. Everything went to shit without her. I spilled my guts to Atheist during my lowest points, where I cradled my revolver in my lap, waiting for the courage to pull the trigger. He would whine and hop up beside me. I would tell him why I wanted to die, and he would remind me what I wanted to live for. I sat on the bed, rustling Atheist's collar to remind myself he was really here.

"Let's play a game," Gia said. "I'll tell you one fucked-up thing from my childhood, and you tell me one."

What a game. "It's too early for this shit, Gia." I moved to scoot away from her, but she grabbed my arm and cleared her throat.

"When I was eight, I was abducted for ransom by this skeevy 'gang,' if you could even call them that. That was just the first of many times men have hurt me." Her lip quivered slightly.

Gia's admission made my heart drop. How could she even let me fuck her the way I did? Didn't it remind her of her past? Every so often, her touch would send me back into the moment where a heavy hand raced up my thigh. The memories would rattle me, only calmed by the warm embrace of her mouth or pussy.

Ah, it made sense.

"Why . . ." I paused, unsure how to word what I wanted to ask. "Why do you want me fuck you like that, then? The things you have me say—"

"I don't know. I'm not a damn psychologist, but I'm assuming it comes from being made to feel that way for so long. It somehow transformed from something that bothered me into a thing that made me come."

"Do you think of them? Any of them?" I asked. From the corner of my eye, I saw her eyebrow lift.

"Sometimes, when we fuck." Gia rubbed Atheist's cheek. "But not like you think. It's almost like a big fuck you to them. I can still enjoy sex while their nails rake my brain. When you're behind me and you ignore me, their hot breath rolls over me and reminds me they're still there. That they still have a piece of me with them. But then your voice shakes me out of it, and it just feels that much better when I remember you're the one inside me and I'm safe."

"There's no safety here. Not in this life."

"I feel like I kind of know what happened to you, Enzo. Not the details, but the way you responded to me just now. It's the same way you get sometimes when I touch you. Something similar happened to you, huh?" She pulled me into her, but I grabbed her wrists and pushed her away.

"None of that shit happened to me," I lied. Even though she already knew the truth, I had to lie.

Atheist whined louder, sensing the change in my mood. He always knew when the shrapnel of painful emotions pierced me.

"It's okay if it happened. It's not your—"

"Nothing happened to me! Let it fucking go, Gia!" I climbed out of bed. What happened to me didn't mold me like it had molded her. I was a product of my own choices, not everyone else's.

Gia

I PUSHED TOO HARD, I thought as I heard the shower running. I just wanted him to open up to me. My mind had wandered, unearthing the memories I'd buried. I knew bringing it up would remind me of every damn time I tried to forget, but it was worth the risk. He was suffering with a hurt that I recognized in myself, a trauma that took a piece of me that I wouldn't get back. Like planks missing from a wooden bridge, only the bridge led to my soul, giving me no choice but to turn around and embrace my demons. That pain mocked me eternally, never letting me have true happiness. I had to be brave enough to leap and hope the person on the other side was willing to catch me. I'd been trying to jump, but Enzo wasn't ready to be the other person. If he would just open up to me, he could see I was ready and willing to catch *him*.

"Sorry," Enzo said. I hadn't heard him turn the shower off, too busy wading through the shit within my head. He brushed a hand through his hair, a towel tied around his waist.

"For what?" I furrowed my brows at him, wrapping the sheet around me protectively.

"Snapping at you . . . about things." Enzo came over, grabbed the back of my head, and pulled me into him. I let my cheek rest on the taut muscles of his abdomen, still warm and wet from his shower. "Things happened to me too, Gia. Stuff I couldn't begin to talk about. I'm just not there yet. But I'm here now." His lips fell to mine, letting me breathe in his pain.

His hand wrapped around my neck, and he pulled me closer with a growl. "I'm sorry I fuck you the way I do. You're the worst drug, and I just want to overdose on you." His words were so genuine that it made heat rise behind my eyes.

"Enzo—"

"Don't get too flattered. I still think you're a batshit crazy bitch." He smirked as he pulled away from me.

"Yeah, and you're still a dick." I shrugged at him with a grin. I didn't know if we were meant to love or hate each other, but it felt right to ride the line between both extremes. With a playful gaze, he dropped his towel, beckoning me to my knees with his eyes. We may have hurt each other, but we pleased each other just as much.

Chapter Twenty-Five

Enzo

Gia sat in the driver's seat and crossed her legs as she buckled her seatbelt. "I can't believe we're doing this."

"Me either, but Bullseye set this whole thing up. Supposed to be an easy drop. My guys already got it over the state lines, so now we just need to get them home," I said as I pulled out of the garage. It was gloomy outside, with a stagnant humidity that made my skin feel wet. Or maybe it was just the nerves causing sweat to leach from me.

"If it's so easy, why isn't he doing it?"

"Bullseye got called to handle another matter," I said, unwilling to answer any more questions about this. I didn't want to do it either, but there we were.

"How much are we picking up? Enough for you to take the damn SUV?"

I rolled my eyes at her, my fingers grasping the steering wheel so hard my knuckles were paper white. Dealing with guns was something I was vehemently against. I'd lost good people because of it. Like drugs, the elusive nature and desperation behind that trade made it that much more dangerous. It almost seemed more perilous than drugs, their trade depending on the use of those stolen guns with serial numbers filed off to hide their paper trail.

We pulled up to the docks, the water lapping at the shoreline in front of us. I put the car in park and we got out, letting the stagnant heat embrace us. I ushered Gia behind me and we walked toward the warehouse, our steps echoing on the wooden planks. The scent of fish lingered in the air. Aside from a few employees in blue coveralls and a man in a suit, his jacket slung over his shoulder, the marina was empty.

"Enzo Viglione?" the man said as we approached, rising from the case he was sitting on.

"Yes, I never got your name," I said with a hint of suspicion. I didn't recognize the man, and I knew everyone in this game.

"That's not really important." He flashed a smile as he shrugged on his coat.

"I don't do business with ghosts."

"Well, you'll have to this time." He gestured toward the large wooden crate beside him.

I felt all types of uncomfortable about the transaction, and sweat collected at the small of my back where the sun aimed its ugly rays behind me.

"Where's it going?" I asked as I walked closer to the crate. I gestured to one of the men in blue, who used a pry bar to break open the lip. My eyebrows cocked at the contents—more rifles than I even anticipated. With another gesture, the man in blue nailed the lid down again. I motioned toward the men to carry the crate to the SUV, and they hurried to lift it. My eyes locked on the man, who hadn't moved since we'd arrived. "Where is it going?" I asked again, more firmly.

"Did they tell you nothing?" The man chuckled as he lifted an eyebrow.

"No." I shook my head, maintaining my glare. My heartbeat picked up speed and thumped against my chest.

"The drop off is Malchikov Ilych," the man said with a humorless laugh as he handed over a piece of paper with an address on it. Malchikov was the boss of the biggest and most influential Russian family.

Fucking Bullseye. There was only one thing I hated dealing with more than firearms, and it was the Russians.

By the time I looked up again, the man was gone.

"Well, fuck," I said with a heavy exhale.

"What's wrong?"

"The guns are going to the fucking Russians. The Ilyich family." I crumpled the paper and stuck it in my pocket.

"We can't . . . Enzo, that's way out of either of our realms. Even your family doesn't fuck around with their organization."

"I know that!" I snapped, making her recoil. "What can I do? I got the guns, and now I have to deliver them."

I grabbed Gia's arm, and we walked toward the SUV. My thoughts raced. I'd seen the violence tightly interwoven into their business, and they made my family look like saints. They were strong and ruthless, and it made them excellent businessmen. Kindness never got you far in the lifestyle.

We drove toward the address burning a hole in my pocket.

"What are we going to do?" Gia asked, and I couldn't have given her an answer if I tried. I had no fucking idea.

"*We* aren't doing anything. *You* are going to stay in the

fucking car." My voice was firm enough to make her sit back without rebuttal. "This family is as dangerous as they come, and I want you to stay hidden, alright?"

"Fine," she said with a pout of her lips.

I looked out the windshield, craning my neck at the huge mansion in front of us. The men guarding the property weren't anything like the guards at Gia's house. Tattooed hands wrapped around their rifles.

"Get in the backseat, Gia."

"But—"

"Now, Gia. For once, can you just do what I ask?"

She let out a huff, clambered into the back seat, and flattened herself to the floor.

I pulled up to the gate's tall black bars and lowered the window as a gruff man peered inside.

"Pochemu ty zdes'?" the man asked.

I didn't speak Russian, but I could at least tell them I couldn't. "Ya ne govoryu po-russki."

The man cocked his head, a smirk creeping across his face. "Why . . . you . . . here?" he asked in broken English.

"Guns." I gestured toward the back of the SUV.

The man had no issue understanding *that* word. He returned to the booth, speaking Russian as he radioed us in. The metal gate crept open.

"Prodolzhat'," he said with a wave of his hand.

I parked the car at the top of the driveway, looking around at the mansion's old stone structure. "Stay here, Gia."

Men swarmed me as I exited the car, and everyone was armed as fuck. *Seems like they have enough guns already.* I lifted my hands as they approached and took positions around the circular driveway. Men even came out of the damn bushes surrounding the arching staircase of the massive home.

A well-dressed man with gray hair approached behind them, shielded by bodies and weaponry. The man spoke in thick Russian to his colleagues. The men dropped their rifle barrels, though their hands remained wrapped around them.

"Mr. Viglione." The man spoke perfect English, though his accent peppered his words.

"Malchikov Ilych." I smiled as I stepped forward and shook his tattoo-covered hand. A piece of a thief's star crept from beneath his unbuttoned dress shirt.

"You brought the guns? What happened to Bullseye?"

"You know Bullseye?" I asked with a cock of my eyebrow.

"Oh, yes." He smiled and grabbed my shoulder. "Come, let's have a drink. My men will take care of the rest." Malchikov motioned toward his men.

I looked back at the SUV. "I can't stay, Malchikov."

"Nonsense, come." He turned to walk toward the house, and one of his men pushed me along from behind. Clearly the invitation was not a choice.

I followed him through the large winding corridors of the mansion as he conversed with his men in their native language. Laughter echoed off the walls as they spoke. He brought me to a large open room with plastic laid over the concrete floors. Cars lined the wall in front of a huge garage door. The man who still had his arm on me had a rose wrapped around a dagger on his forearm. I didn't know the meanings of all the various images etched in ink, but I knew enough to know I didn't want to find out.

A mechanical whirr filled the silence, and the garage door crept open. My eyes widened as I saw Gia being pulled into the room between two men. In typical Gia fashion, she spewed obscenities from her lips. I tried to run to her, but the men held me back.

"What do we have here?" Malchikov said in a tone that dripped with excited curiosity, like someone just brought in a gift for him.

Not my girl. Not Gia.

"No!" I said through clenched teeth.

Malchikov met the men in the middle of the room as Gia thrashed toward him with fire in her eyes.

"Who's this little kotenok?" he said with a low voice as he brushed a hand through Gia's hair.

The weight of the revolver on my hip leapt to the forefront of my mind, and I longed for it. I looked around at the rifles in the room. We were completely outgunned and outnumbered. "She's mine," I said as the men held me back.

"Oh, is that so?" Malchikov fisted Gia's hair, making her whimper. She had no fear in her expression, only annoyance. He wrapped a hand around her waist and pulled her into him.

"Fuck off," Gia snarled.

Malchikov turned toward the men with a laugh as he grabbed her face. "Ah, she's got a mouth on her."

"We brought you your guns, Malchikov. We have no more business with you," I said.

"Oh, you think I'm going to kill you two?" Malchikov laughed. "No, no, I have no interest in killing you. I just had to make sure the goods were as expected." His eyes lingered on Gia's body. "But this little kotenok was not expected."

"Leave her!" I yelled, my voice straining as muscled arms held me in place.

"You guys will be on your way." He looked back at me.

"After I'm done with her." A sadistic grin crawled across his face.

"No!" I broke free, only to take a punch to my gut that brought me to my knees. I reached for my revolver, but a kick knocked me onto my back.

"Enzo, stop!" Gia shouted.

My chest heaved as I tried to catch my breath. I turned onto my belly and looked up at her. His dirty hands were on her, racing over her hips.

"I'm fine, I'll be fine," she said with confidence. She knew as well as I did how precarious this situation was. Fighting would only get one or both of us killed.

⁓

Gia

Enzo continued to crawl toward me, taking every hit that kept knocking him back. I stood at a crossroads that made my heart ache. I could fuck this foul man and save us both, or we could fight an unwinnable battle. It wasn't the first time—and most likely wouldn't be the last time—I had to barter with my body.

"Bring her to my room," Malchikov said to his men.

They pushed me toward the door, and I heard Enzo's strained voice behind me. They led me down hallways until we reached a large wooden door with intricate inlay patterns. The men opened the door and dragged me inside. The bedroom was bigger than anything in either of our homes, and I gasped at the size of it. Expensive furniture and various trappings decorated the large space. The door closed behind me and made me jump. Malchikov's hand landed on my ass, and he growled as he pulled me into him, pushing his men's hands away. They backed off and blocked the door.

"I won't fight you, so they don't need to watch," I said as I gestured toward the men.

"I don't trust a woman like you." He smirked as he brushed his hand through my hair. "You are a lioness, kotenok, and I know you would bite me."

His gray eyes poured into mine, a shade close to the salt and pepper color of his hair. With his thin face and high cheekbones, he wasn't an unattractive man, but he was still a vile one. He began to unbutton his dress shirt, the fabric spreading to reveal a taut and inked stomach. The words etched into his skin were faded with age and difficult to read. There were stars on his chest.

He pulled me into him as he yanked up my skirt, bunching it at my hips. His hand raced between my thighs and pried beneath my panties. Thoughts of Enzo ripped into my mind, causing guilt to twist my gut. As he slipped his fingers inside me, he unbuttoned his pants. He pushed me onto the bed, and the soft fabric caused goosebumps to rise on my back. He crawled between my legs, worked his zipper down, and pressed the heat of his cock against me. I felt numb as he kissed me, his lips spreading on mine, which remained tightly closed. He thrust inside me, and I let myself react for only a moment before I receded back into my mind. His thrusts were hurried but deep, sometimes grabbing me from within my head and dragging me to the surface as he took his frustration out on me. His intensity made my stomach tighten as pleasure crept into places it didn't belong. His hand reached down and grabbed my ass, pulling me against him. The sounds of his body hitting mine were nauseatingly loud, radiating between my ears. I kept any moans deep within my throat as his breath rolled over the sweaty skin of my neck.

"Fuck, malyshka . . ." he growled against me as his thrusts slowed and became uneven. He reached down and gripped himself as he pulled out of me, painting me with the remnants of his excitement. Despite not wanting any of this, his receding cock still gave my body a moment of longing. He stood and pulled his pants up, buttoning them as he disappeared into the bathroom. Malchikov returned with a warm towel and allowed me to clean myself up. He reached out a hand to help me to my feet, but I only snatched my skirt into place as I glared at him.

"You may have been kind, but that doesn't make this any less fucked up," I said.

He wrapped his hand around my neck. "I always get what I want, malyshka." After a fleeting kiss, he left the room without another word. The door closed and the reality of what had just happened weighed me down.

Chapter Twenty-Six

Enzo

I couldn't even look at Gia as her leg shook beside me, and she couldn't bear to look at me, either. I was so angry that heat rose from my skin. The thoughts of her being fucked by another man nauseated me. I wasn't mad at her. How could I be? We knew we had no other way out of that. Not alive, at least. The only person I *wasn't* mad at was her. I was pissed at Malchikov, Bullseye and, most importantly, myself. I shouldn't have brought her.

"Gia?" I tried to get her attention by dropping my hand to her thigh, but she flinched and pushed me away.

During the silent drive home, she sniffled every so often, but she hid any tears from me. Her leg had stopped shaking by the time we pulled into the garage. Without looking back at me, she climbed out of the car and ran inside. I chased after her but crashed into the broad chest of Silvio.

"What the hell happened?" Silvio said in a gruff voice.

"Not now, Silvio."

I tried to walk past him, but he grabbed my shoulder

and pushed me toward the library. He slammed me against the wall the moment we stepped foot inside.

"What the hell happened?"

"The fucking Russians happened," I snarled as I pushed him back. "This is why I don't fuck with guns!"

"Everything was delivered fine, and the money came as agreed upon," Silvio said with a shrug.

I grabbed his shoulders and lifted them by the fabric of his jacket. "Did you fucking know?"

"Know what?" Silvio asked with a callous grin.

I reared my arm back and punched him in the face, my hand sliding along his oily skin. "You fucking knew we were delivering to Malchikov, didn't ya?"

Silvio faltered from the blow, touching his cheek with his hand as he chuckled at me. "Did you think I would just let you two be together? Like nothing? Like we haven't been fighting for more than one lifetime?"

"Fuck you!" I shouted as I shoved him again.

"We found Lorenzo's body, you know," Silvio said with a cock of his eyebrow.

"So? Who the fuck cares about him? He's nothing to me."

"You wouldn't know anything about how he died?" Silvio asked, a hint of accusation in his tone.

"Nah, ask one of the many enemies he created for himself. He was wanted citywide, Pops, and I told you not to bring him back in." I stood tall, my muscles rigid.

"Mm-hmm." Silvio nodded his head. He looked as if he had more to say to me but thought better of it. Good choice.

"Are we done here?" I snarled.

"Don't forget to get me my stuff." He tapped his nose and smiled.

I wanted to tell him to get his own damn drugs, but I

thought better of saying more. I scoffed before leaving him to baby his cheek by himself.

My heart thumped against my chest. Silvio sent us into the wolf's den, knowing they'd pounce on Gia. *Fucking piece of shit.* I raced upstairs to find Gia. When I got to my room and nudged Atheist away with my knee, I heard the shower running in the bathroom. Part of me wanted to go in there and comfort her, but I worried my anger would spill onto the one person who didn't deserve it.

I'd experienced something like this only once before, and I handled it way worse back then. I was dating a broad from Long Island, and she was the opposite of Gia in every way. My lifestyle caught up to us one night, and I ended up bound and watching two men from one of our rival families —who Silvio no doubt pissed off—rape her in front of me. The screams would forever be etched into my memory, and the way she looked at me as if I was to blame . . . well, there was no way I wasn't. Back then, I treated her like it had been her fault and that I couldn't be with her because of it. Like she was too *used*. That wasn't wholly the truth, though. I couldn't sleep with her without remembering what I saw. I refused to make Gia feel that way, no matter how mad I was.

By the time I shook myself from my memories, she'd stepped out of the bathroom. She was already dressed, and she looked away from me as she walked toward the bed. I followed her, trying to get in bed with her, but she shrugged away from me.

Please don't push me away. "Gia," I whispered, as if talking to a scared animal.

"Leave me alone," she said as she slipped into bed and turned over.

I couldn't leave her alone. I wouldn't let her sit on this

guilt all night. I grabbed her arm and tugged her toward me. She finally looked up at me, her dark eyes rounded with sadness. I straddled her and pinned her arms above her head to stop her from flailing as she tried to push me away.

"Listen to me!" I said through clenched teeth. "I am not mad at you, Gia. I'm not even upset with you. I'm the one you should be upset with, and I'm so sorry!"

Her lips trembled. "I . . . Enzo . . ."

I released her hands and dropped beside her, wrapping my arms around her. "What happened?" Though I didn't want to know, I needed to hear it.

Her body melted against mine as the tension poured out of her.

"Tell me, Gia." I grabbed her chin and forced her eyes to look at mine. "Did he hurt you?"

She shook her head.

"Was it just him?"

She recoiled at my words, as if being tossed into the pit of a memory. She nodded. It broke my heart to see her feeling so weak. It was so uncharacteristic of her, and it was hard to witness.

She finally broke the silence with a trembling voice. "I just let it happen. I didn't even put up a fight." She shook her head as she spoke, her eyes glazing over.

I pulled her into me. "I wouldn't have wanted you to fight. You did everything you had to do."

Her body shivered violently, and I pulled the blanket over her. I brushed the hair from her face, kissing her cheek before resting my face against hers and inhaling her scent.

"Am I mad?" I continued. "Yes, but not at you. I'm fucking jealous and possessive, and I can't stand that he got to have you." I couldn't tell her how possessive I actually felt. I wanted to fuck her back in the car, claim her as my own again. But she was hurt, and I couldn't let myself be me.

"I just feel dirty."

"No, Gia!" Her words reminded me of that girl from Long Island, and it caused my voice to rise too sharply. "There is nothing you could do to be dirty."

"Yes there is, Enzo!" she raised her voice back at me, snarling my name.

"No—"

"My body liked it," she said so quietly I almost didn't hear her. But I heard enough of it. My jaw dropped at her confession.

Now *that* made me angry, though my mind argued with me about how I enjoyed some shit that happened to me too. Sometimes our bodies betray us.

I reached for her face, and she flinched as if she thought I would hit her. I would never. "Did you come?" I asked, and it made me curse myself under my breath. That was too much. I just needed to know. That fucking Russian took something that belonged to me, and most importantly to her, and I needed to know just how much of her he got. Did he feel how tight she got when she came? Did he get to hear how her moans sounded?

"No," she said with a quick shake of her head. I wished I could tell her about things that happened to me, to make her understand why I was the way I was. We were both too used to trauma like that. That was the sad part.

"Do you want to?"

Her gaze shot to mine. The twist in her lips made me certain she would smack me, and I probably deserved it. My desire to fuck her again, to be the last one inside her, was too intense. I wouldn't force her to fuck me, but I was salivating over her.

She shook her head, but the shaking became slower and less intense until it was merely a shallow sway.

"It's okay if you don't, babygirl." I pulled her into me again. I wanted her so bad that I ached, but she had something precious taken from her once more and I wasn't going to give her anything unless it was going to give her something back.

⬩

Gia

I DIDN'T KNOW what I wanted. There was a guilty ache in my gut because I'd wanted more from Malchikov. My heart and mind were horrified, but my body still reacted to his touch. *That's so fucked up.* I wanted Enzo, but how could I let him fuck me while that man was still a black mark between my legs? The only way to calm the ache was to let him take me, and my fingers grazed Enzo's chest as I worked his buttons down. He looked down at me with a sultry smirk crossing his lips.

It was all the invitation he needed, and he wrapped his hand around my neck as he laid me on my back and spread my legs with his knees. He let his shirt fall to the floor and grabbed the waistband of my shorts, tugging them down my thighs, his eyes still on me, watching for signs to stop. His black pants did nothing to hide how hard he was, the bulging fabric straining against his length. The sound of his zipper sliding along its track made me shiver. His cock grazed my inner thighs, thicker and bigger than Malchikov, but dripping with the same desire. Enzo leaned over me to kiss me, and his heat brought my mind back to being beneath that Russian piece of shit. Enzo stopped the moment he sensed my body tense.

"Babygirl," he whispered. His hands hovered over me as if he didn't know if he should touch me at all.

"I'm okay," I said as I wrapped my legs around him and pulled him into me.

He looked at me, hesitating before he reached down and put himself inside me. The moment he was in me, I felt the guilt race through my veins. I gasped and felt the urge to push him away. Enzo noticed every subtle change in my body language.

"I can stop," he said with a low growl to his words, which didn't seem too convincing. He buried his face against my neck. "I just wanted to make sure you knew you were mine. I don't care if that Russian bastard fucked you. I don't even care if he made you come. The only thing that matters is that you are fucking mine."

Enzo's words melted me. I put my arms around his neck and brought my mouth to his ear. "I'm yours," I whispered, my words making him react with his hips.

He let go of his resolve and apprehension as his hips pounded mine. I arched my back, heaving my chest toward him as his powerful, hungry thrusts tore at me. Enzo reached down and rubbed me, his warm fingers gliding against my clit.

"I can feel you tightening. Are you gonna come for me, Gia?" He looked down at me with a loose-lipped smile that made the dimples above his lips more pronounced.

I whimpered as I nodded, burying my face in his chest. I thought he might stop my ascent, hold me back from reaching the top like he always did. But his fingers didn't slow or hasten. He just rubbed me until I bucked against his hand.

"Come for me," he growled against my ear as his belly drew in, his posture tensing. I came so hard that I pushed him over the edge at the same moment, and a pleasure that was almost too intense to recover from pulsed through us. He made sure his cock was the only thing I could think about.

Chapter Twenty-Seven

Enzo

I made Gia wait in the car. I wouldn't leave her at home, but I sure as fuck couldn't bring her inside with me. The stale club air welcomed me the moment I walked through the doors. I pushed past topless women and batted away their flirty touches as I headed toward the back door. Everyone turned toward me as the door slammed shut behind me. All the usuals. I looked around the back room of the club. A stain on the floor still marked where Rudy had been shot.

Pure anger emitted from me in waves and made Bullseye stand, pushing his chair out as he did. His hand rested on his pistol.

"I ain't gonna kill you, ya piece of shit!" I yelled. "I just wanna fucking talk!"

Kenny leapt from the big round table in the middle of the room to hold me back, but I pushed against his chest.

"I got nothing to say, Enzo." Bullseye shrugged his shoulders as he sat again.

"What do you mean you got nothing to say? You set us up! You let Gia—" I stopped myself, the words catching in my throat. Gia had enough going against her without them knowing she slept with the Russian, even if it wasn't her choice.

"I didn't set up shit! I thought you knew who it was for. I told your father—"

"Silvio is a piece of shit," I snarled. "You know the Russians are ruthless, and you let me bring Gia there!"

Bullseye narrowed his eyes. "You weren't supposed to bring her. A girl like that? Fuck, she would be—"

I slipped past Kenny and charged toward Bullseye, but another couple of men held me back. "Tread lightly," I said with a sneer. I slammed my fist on the table. "I told you I didn't want to deal with guns, and you told me this was an easy drop. We hardly made it outta there alive!" I pointed toward him, my glare locked on his. "Which brings me to my follow-up question. How the fuck do they know you? It was clear you guys have done business before."

"What business my family has done has nothing to do with you," Bullseye said with a humorless laugh. "Why make an enemy out of the Russians when we don't have to?"

"You fucking tell *me* next time you come up with any bright ideas to deal with the Russians, because if I see Malchikov again, he's a dead man."

There was a knock on the door behind me and it shook my gaze away from Bullseye when it opened. "What?" I hissed as I turned around and saw one of the dancers. Two men in suits stood behind her, and I cleared my throat, turning on my suave business persona like I'd flipped a light switch. "What can I help you with?"

The men behind me stood in front of the bloodstain on the floor to block the view from the strangers.

The two agents waved off the half-naked blonde, watching her walk away with a quick side glance. "May we come in?"

"You already are, no?" I glared at her receding form for a moment before gesturing with my arm to come inside.

They closed the door behind them, silencing the loud music from the club. "I'm Agent Dowell and this is Agent Rocco." The blond officer pointed to the dark-haired man beside him.

Rocco. The Rocco's? Fucking dude's a fed now? Talk about swapping sides.

Agent Rocco eyed me with the same recognition. "I'm going to just pretend you all have legal permits to carry those firearms," Rocco said with a snide smile. "Listen, we know what you do here. We know half those bitches out there didn't choose to be—"

"We—"

"Well, here's the thing. I don't really fucking care what you guys do in this dump. This little visit is merely a formality. That is, if you're willing to help us turn a blind eye . . . or four." Rocco smirked as he gestured toward himself and his partner.

He didn't switch sides at all. He's just playing the game from a whole new field. I was silent too long, trying to weigh the options.

"Are you really considering paying these goons?" Bullseye piped up from his chair behind me.

Rocco turned toward him with fire in his eyes. "We have enough evidence on this place to put you all away for a fuck ton of time. I don't think you have much of a choice."

"How do we know you have anything on us?" Bullseye quipped.

"We have fraudulent passports and mugshots of ladies

who sang like the little birds they are. You remember Leodine, don't you? Small blonde-haired French—"

"Yeah, I know who she is," I interrupted. Leodine was incredible on her knees, but get her talking and she'd spill her guts about anyone.

When Bullseye scoffed, Rocco turned back toward me with a smile. "So, how about it?"

"You're a goddamn disgrace to us, Rocco," I said as I went to the safe and squatted to unlock it.

"I want to tell you not to hate the player, but this is my fucking game," he said with faked pleasantry.

"Yeah, yeah. How much to get you well-dressed pieces of shit off my back?" I asked as I turned my head to look at them. They whispered to each other. "Today! I got shit to do."

"Give us two hundred grand," Rocco said with a shrug.

"Two-fucking-hundred." I scoffed as I pulled out cash and loaded it onto the counter. I spun the dial until I heard the *click* that let me know it had locked. I stood and gestured at the money and Bullseye. "You fucking deal with this!" I snapped as I went to leave out the back door.

"Have a good day, Mr. Viglione!" I heard from behind me.

"Choke on a dick, Rocco," I called back with a wave as I slammed the door.

Gia leapt out of the car when she saw me. "I saw the agents! Isn't the one—"

"Yeah, one of us," I said with a shake of my head.

"Bribe?"

"Oh yeah, and a decent-sized one, too." I shrugged. "The Roccos were fucking bottom feeders, so I'm not surprised."

Gia stepped into me and put her hand down the front of my pants. I grabbed her wrist and pulled it out.

"What? You're frustrated." She looked at me and bit her lip.

"I ain't gonna fuck you any time I'm upset, Giovanna," I told her with a hint of a smirk before dragging her toward the car.

My hands pushed her skirt up before we even made it inside, exposing the tan skin of her perfect ass to the entire parking lot. I didn't care, and neither did she. We couldn't even get the door closed before we were too hungry for each other. I took her then and there, with her back on the warm leather of my backseat. I heard a wolf whistle and the sound of Rocco's voice behind me. I pulled out, tucking myself into my pants as Gia hesitated for a moment, her pussy glistening with her excitement, before covering herself with her skirt. I turned around and saw Rocco, his head cocked, a tight smile on his face. The jealousy was clear in his expression.

"Really, Enzo? Sylvester's daughter?" Rocco said with a curl of his lip.

Gia stood and adjusted her skirt.

"Good luck with that, sweetheart," Rocco said to Gia. He opened the car door and looked back at her one more time. "Quite the shame," he said with a kiss blown her way.

"Let's finish this at home." I smacked her ass, grabbing the full flesh of her in a frustrated grasp. She pouted her lips for a moment before nodding and getting into the car. Rocco had my money, but I had something worth so much more to dive into every night.

Chapter Twenty-Eight

Gia

"We are not going to get drugs for your father!" I shook my head.

"Silvio has a voracious coke habit," Enzo said with a smirk. He put the car in drive and pulled out of the garage. The sun pierced our eyes through the windshield, and I slammed the visor down.

"I really don't want to do this. We don't deal with drugs for a reason."

"We ain't dealing with nothing. Just picking it up for personal use."

"Personally or professionally, that's still dealing with drugs." I rolled my eyes at him. The memory of what happened on our last rendezvous was still fresh in my mind.

"Gia, stop. It's fine. We've been using the same people for years."

I scoffed and folded my arms over my chest. We drove just out of the city, toward an unsuspecting home within a community neighborhood. The house we parked in front of was in a fucking cul-de-sac, for Christ's sake. Enzo parked the car and came over to open my door. My eyes were still stuck on the colonial house in front of us.

"This doesn't look like a drug house," I said as I looked around the peaceful neighborhood with children's toys littering almost every lawn.

I followed Enzo as he rang the doorbell and waited. A middle-aged man nearly pulled us into the house as soon as he opened the door. He looked like your average dad type, and there were pictures of him and his family looking completely . . . not like drug lords.

"The usual, Enzo?" the man said as he put on a pair of oven mitts and pulled a steaming-hot pan out of the oven.

Is this real life right now?

"Yeah, Harry, that's fine," Enzo said.

"The supply cost has gone up a bit since we last got a shipment," Harry said in a rush of words as he nearly dropped the pan onto the top of the stove.

"It's fine, whatever it costs."

"Who's your lady friend?" Harry leaned his head into the doorway.

"This is Gia," Enzo said with a proud smile that made my cheeks flush with heat.

"You're very pretty, miss." He smiled at me. "Do you want some drugs? I have heroin, E, coke, as you know, and . . ." He counted them off in his head. "I think I have a little acid left."

I had to bite my lip to control the laughter at this drug-peddling father with an apron on in his suburban fucking neighborhood.

"I'll try some coke," I said with a shrug of my shoulders.

"No, you won't." Enzo narrowed his eyes at me and shook his head. "No thank you, Harry, we're good."

I started to speak, but Enzo's commanding stare made me bite my tongue.

Harry came out of the back room with a duffle bag and spread it open to show Enzo the wrapped bags of coke. Enzo smiled as he exchanged the money for the bag and gestured for me to move toward the door.

"Nice to meet you," I said with a smile as we left.

"Your dad is going to use *all* that coke?" I closed the trunk after Enzo placed the duffle bag inside. "I don't understand why I couldn't try some."

He grabbed my face. "This coke is shit, absolutely terrible quality. Harry is very nice, but I have no idea what kind of rank place he gets this shit from. I ain't getting that man nothing better, but if I were to let you do something like that, I would make sure you had the finest." He smirked and leaned in to kiss me. My chest flushed with heat at his words. "If you want it, I can get it for you, but it's not going to be this boric acid cut shit."

It had started to get dark by the time we drove toward home. The sun dodged beneath the tree line, awaiting its descent past the horizon. We drove by a mansion illuminated by yellow-tinged lights around the perimeter. I looked at it with a cock of my head.

"Why do I recognize that house?" I gestured toward it.

Enzo ducked his head and looked at it, his lips tightening. "That was the Ricci's home," he said flatly.

"Was?"

"Yeah, the family pretty much dismantled after their pops died. A shame too because if we could find any of them right about now, they'd be dead for narcing on us." Enzo shook his head. "To this day, I don't understand why they pitted us against each other at the docks."

"Maybe taking one of us down meant taking us both

down somehow. Causing us to fight and get sloppy was probably the only way the Riccis could have had a chance at the top."

"Are any of us really at the top?" Enzo said with a smirk. He was right. We always felt like we had one foot in the grave and the other trying to trip the feds and keep them down as long as possible.

"I worry about my father and Ro." I dropped my gaze. "Have they said anything about me?"

"We haven't heard a thing from your family." His words were certain, and I knew they were true. My family had no reason to try to get me home yet. "Do you want me to bring you back?"

"Home?" I asked with wide eyes.

"Yeah. I can bring you back."

"I don't . . . I don't think I want to. Not yet, at least." I watched him as the shadows danced across his face, the headlights reflecting off the oncoming cars. He reached over and put his hand on my thigh, squeezing it.

Enzo

I WAS RELIEVED Gia didn't want to go back home yet. It felt like she was already home. I touched the soft skin of her thigh, rubbing my hand up and down.

"I won't keep you here if you don't want to stay with me." I glanced at her, and she melted into the seat at my touch.

"I want to," she said with a soft moan. She was as insatiable as me, in some ways maybe even more so.

She responded to my touch by scooting down and spreading her thighs. I smirked at her before moving my hand up until it nestled against her. My fingers pushed her panties aside as they spread and rubbed her clit. I pushed inside her, causing her to grip the armrest. She bucked against my hand and grinded against my palm. Just as she was about to come, I snatched my hand away with a sadistic grin on my face. She groaned. Her wetness coated my fingers, and I brought them to my lips and licked them. Her taste intoxicated me.

"I'm going to fuck you with my tongue the moment we get home." She moaned at my words. "I haven't decided if I'll let you come, though."

"Why are you like this?" She smoothed her skirt down, covering her thighs.

I shrugged at her, but I knew why. I loved to have all the control. I loved to hear her begging and pleading for what I alone could give her. Having all that under my control was addictive, and she'd have to get used to it if she wanted to be with me in any capacity. I would always fuck her mind as much as her body.

Her leg was shaking by the time we pulled into the garage, and she was out of the car the moment I put it in park. I chased after her before remembering the drugs in the car. With a groan, I ran back and opened the trunk, grabbing the pale green duffle bag. When I rushed into the house, I handed the bag to one of the armed men beside the door without a word.

I followed Gia's scent to my room and found her in my t-shirt with no panties on, the cuffs of her ass visible beneath the thin fabric. She rolled onto her back and smiled at me. This girl.

"Come here," I commanded, my voice low and sultry.

She protested, and a flash of her eyes told me what she wanted.

"I fucking said come here!" I raised my voice and pointed to the floor at my feet.

She shook her head, making me cross the room and grab her by her hair. I helped her to her feet, and then down to her knees.

"I don't like it when you don't fucking listen," I said as I worked the button and zipper of my pants with the hand not entwined in her hair. The weight of my revolver helped my pants fall to the ground where they belonged. I kicked my shoes off and stepped out of the mound of fabric.

She was a work of art at my feet, looking up at me with eyes just as hungry for me as mine were for her. The way she bit her lips made me want to shove my dick between them, and I would. I'd fuck that pretty mouth of hers until she begged me to stop. The problem was, she'd never beg me to stop. Not Gia. I'd have no choice but to choke her with my dick until I came down her throat.

But she preferred it inside her pussy.

I pulled the front of my boxers down, exposing myself in front of her face. Her eyes always widened at the sight of me. As I fisted her hair, I knew just how much I was going to stretch her throat, and with that very intimate knowledge, I shoved myself into her mouth. Her lips wrapped around me in a warm embrace that sent shivers up my spine. I held her by the hair as I fucked her face, her gags making me throb.

"Enzo," she said during a quick reprieve when I pulled my dick from her mouth to let her catch her breath. Drool dripped down her chin, and smears of black makeup trailed down her cheeks from her tears.

"What, babygirl?" I asked as I brushed her hair from her face.

"I want you to come in my mouth." She bit her lip as she looked up at me.

Her request took me off guard. I didn't expect something like that from Giovanna Silvani. Not self-directed, at least. I would expect to command her, engage in the ensuing bratty fight as she refused, and then she'd let me take her throat anyway.

"You sure?" I asked as I stroked myself.

She nodded and took me into her mouth again, sucking as she used her hand on me. I let her take the wheel and drive. If she was going to take my come, I'd let her work it out of me.

I closed my eyes and listened to the sounds of her mouth. Pleasure balled up in my pelvis, and I moved my hips with her until she had as much as she could take inside her. Even then, I grabbed the back of her head and pulled her an inch deeper.

"I'm going to come, Giovanna," I whispered.

Her mouth continued to ride along me, encouraging me to fill her throat. And I did. Oh, fuck yes, I did. She pulled away from me and swallowed hard, sticking her tongue out at me playfully.

"Now come here," I said as I reached for her hand. Once she was back on her feet, I pushed her backward onto the bed and dropped between her legs. I would take every drop of her into my mouth. It was only fair.

But I had a little plan for her.

I dived into her, brushing her wet excitement with the tip of my tongue. My mouth worked her until she was a trembling mess in front of me, her thighs quivering against my shoulders. She grabbed my hair and tugged, pulling me deeper into her.

"Can I please come?" she pleaded.

"Come for me," I commanded.

Within moments, she shuddered against my touch until my tongue became electric against her. She jerked with every lick, and her thighs tightened around me as she quivered. Her chest rose and heaved as she came. Her hands raced for her pussy, trying to stop my mouth, but unlike what I usually did to her, I was going to make her come until she begged me to *stop*.

Her body twitched in the most delicious ways as she tried to free herself from my tongue. Her pleas were more desperate, as if it was physically hurting her for me to keep tonguing her pussy. She rode out the massive waves of her last orgasm only to hop on the coattails of the next. Before I knew it, she was coming again, violently trembling as she did.

She gripped my hair, trying to pull me away, but I didn't stop. Her pained pleas made me hard all over again. Her hands gripped the sheet, her chest spasming upward.

"Please, Enzo, stop," she begged.

I said I'd make her come until she begged me to stop, but I would make her ride one or two more out.

I pulled away from her, only to whisper over her skin, "You always want me to make you come, right? Be careful what you wish for, Giovanna."

"It literally hurts."

I smirked up at her. "Good."

I slammed my fingers inside her and dropped my face into her drenched pussy. Between my spit and her excitement, she was a slick mess. I fingered her, rubbed my thumb along her clit, and cleaned her up with my tongue until she was nearly crying from the discomfort. I lived for that moment. Her body tensed despite the fierce opposition, and her thighs trembled so hard I had to grab them and hold her still. She came, riding the biggest wave she had yet. I gave her one final lick and climbed over her. My cock pressed against her sensitive skin, making her twitch. Fat beads of sweat slid down her skin, and her chest heaved as if she'd run a marathon. Her thighs tensed the moment my cock touched her clit.

She shook her head. "Please, I can't do it again."

"Oh, babygirl. You can, and you will."

Chapter Twenty-Nine

Gia

The sun dipped toward the horizon as Enzo glanced sideways at me, a grin on his face. I felt unstoppable with him by my side. I reached down and felt for the pistol tucked in my waistband. Feeling the warm metal comforted me. Seagulls took flight as we walked over the threshold dividing the docks from the concrete. They squawked at us, landing with a final angry flap of their wings. The wooden boards creaked as I walked across their worn, peeling surfaces. The sight of the ruined boardwalk made me grateful I'd worn sneakers and not heels. Enzo told me to wear comfortable shoes, just in case. I didn't ask why, because I knew why.

Shit was about to go down.

I spotted Enzo's father at the far end of the dock. He leaned over the railing, puffing on a cigar and staring at a large boat tied to the dock. I looked at Enzo, his face a hard mask, lips pressed tight, eyes narrowed. He noticed me staring at him, tucked me under his arm, and continued walking. Our steps echoed through the stifling silence. Even the water seemed still, as if nature itself was holding its breath.

"Pops," Enzo said, leaning against a beam jutting from the dock. He pulled a cigarette out of his pocket and lit it. The smoke billowed from his clenched lips.

"Took you long enough," Silvio said gruffly as he withdrew the cigar and held it between his fingers. His eyes hovered at my chest as a gross smile crossed his face, making me shiver.

"What we got going on here?" Enzo's head swiveled as he looked around the expansive marina, surveying the scene. There were boats of all different sizes, from tourist ships down to little dinghies. Yachts dotted the docks and rocked against the waves.

"A drop," Silvio said before bringing the cigar to his lips.

"Are we dropping or receiving?" Enzo asked with a deep draw of smoke. I cocked my hip and tried to ignore the thick tension between them.

"Receiving money that needs to be laundered. It comes with a good payout, and we got the businesses to do it," Silvio said with a long exhale. "It seems as though some of the other families are losing their footing, and there's no shortage of business because of it."

Enzo shrugged and threw the cigarette to the ground, smothering it beneath his shoe. I glanced toward the big metal building beside the dock. The sound of a beeping truck was replaced by metal clanging together, as if things were being unloaded.

"Come on," Enzo said toward me, his gaze intense.

Silvio took a puff of his cigar and smirked. "Or she could stay with me."

"Over your dead body, Pops," Enzo said with a side glance toward me. "Come on, Gia."

I followed Enzo, my cheeks hot. "What are we walking into?" I asked as I tried to catch up to his long strides.

"I don't know. We don't typically work with this family." Enzo brushed a hand through his hair.

"Why work with them now?" Everything about this felt uncomfortable.

"Desperation, I guess," Enzo said, metal screeching as he opened the door leading into the cavernous warehouse. The air inside was cold and stagnant, and water dripped from holes in the ceiling. Tools and machinery littered the large building. A mechanical whirr from the far end of the building drew my attention. An uneasiness in my chest washed over me. Something wasn't right.

⌯

Enzo

BACKGROUND NOISE BLANKETED my already hushed steps the closer we came to the back of the building. I stayed close to Gia, especially once I noticed her hand hovering near her hip. I'd never seen her truly scared. She had bigger balls than most of the men I knew.

"Gia," a soft but stern voice said from around the corner, making Gia stop mid-step.

She drew a quick breath, and I pulled her into me. "Dad?" she called toward the sound.

With the tap of dress shoes, her father appeared from around the corner. The graying hair of his thick, wavy locks had been lightly brushed back. Gia ran to her father, and he wrapped her in his arms. I felt a pang of jealousy.

"Gee," Ro said as he came around the corner. He brushed his dark hair back as he looked at me, a tight-lipped expression on his face.

"What are you doing here?" Gia asked with a sharp rise in her tone.

"We've been trying to get you back home for a while now." Ro shot daggers from his eyes at me, and they hit their mark.

I didn't force her to stay.

"What? Really? No one's said . . ." She looked back at me.

Ain't no one said anything to me, either.

"You clearly ain't the Espositos," I said.

"We are not," Sylvester said with a smirk.

Several men hopped out of the truck and walked toward Sylvester. They put their hands on their pistols in near unison. All I had was just me and myself.

I eyed the case of money. "What's with the money, Silvani? I'm guessing you ain't here on business."

Gia stepped back and looked around the room, her gaze shifting between us.

"I want to pay you for the time you've had my daughter, but she's coming home with us," Sylvester said, placing a hand on his hip and grasping the gun tucked in his dress pants.

"With all due respect, sir, Gia can make her own mind up about who she wants to go home with," I said as my gaze caught hers. She looked at the floor, and it made my heart skip a beat.

Sylvester took a step forward and his jaw clenched,

making his temples pulse. "Did she tell you why she was there in the first place?"

"Daddy . . ." Gia said with a shaky voice. She grabbed his arm, a childish tactic that likely always worked for her.

"Do you want to tell him or should I?" Sylvester said to her. She looked up at me, finally meeting my gaze.

"What the fuck is he talking about, Gia?" I snapped, brushing a hand through my hair. *What hasn't she told me?*

"Enzo, I—" she began, but her words halted as if they were caught in her throat.

I felt anger rising in my gut. I had always suspected something was off about this entire thing. *So help me God—*

"She was sent to you for nothing more than inside knowledge on your business," Sylvester said evenly. I inhaled sharply as the anger in my gut began to choke out my lungs. "Do you have the recorder?"

She was breathless with panic. I hadn't ever seen Gia panic.

"No." She shook her head.

Sylvester snapped his head toward her with a glare. "What do you mean, no?"

"I-I broke it," she said with trembling lips.

Ro slapped his thigh. I didn't know if I believed her. Everything, all of it, was a fucking lie.

"Enzo," she called to me.

"Save it, Gia. You should go home." I waved them off, turning from her to walk away. There was no sense staying and arguing. I felt betrayed, and there ain't no coming back from that level of betrayal. I thought I fucking *loved* that bitch. Even the word seemed foreign to me now.

A gunshot rang out and I ducked behind a square metal pole that climbed to the ceiling.

"What the fuck!" Gia screamed. I wasn't sure if she was

upset because someone shot at me or because she might have gotten hurt. I resisted every urge to come out and check on her. My drive to protect her hadn't yet gotten the message that she was a conniving bitch. *Goddamn it, Gia.*

At the sound of the gunshots, Silvio ran in, his pistol drawn. He stood beside me, forcing me between the two.

"Silvani, tell your men to stand down," he commanded with flushed cheeks. He struggled to catch his breath as I peered past the pole. The men behind Sylvester had pistols drawn, and even the man himself had his pistol poised. Gia was a crumpled mess on the ground, holding her ears. She looked up at Silvio, and her mouth dropped open. Sylvester raised his hand and his men lowered their pistols, but Sylvester kept his trained on Silvio.

Silvio's finger curled into the trigger guard, hovering over it. The tension in his body made me certain he would shoot. Silvio would definitely shoot. Sylvester postured, but he wasn't a big bad killer like the rest of us, not unless he had to be.

"Silvio, no!" Gia screamed and got between them, placing her body in front of her father.

I wiped my sweat-soaked hands on my dress pants and crouched as I peered from behind the pole. *He would have no issue taking her out with her father. She was a distraction, after all.*

Silvio always bit into his lip as if he were snarling before he pulled the trigger. He made the familiar motion, and without thinking, I pulled my revolver, aimed, and fired a shot. Screams filled the room. My ears rang with the disorienting buzz of gunfire.

"Fuck!" I yelled as the sound of the Silvani group retreated. Gia cried and pleaded as her family ushered her out.

I ran toward Silvio and spotted a bleeding hole in his gut. The blood flowed freely, and he looked at me with ultimate betrayal. I deserved it. I couldn't let him kill Gia. I could never live with myself. Fuck if I knew why I saved her.

Fuck her.

I stared at him as I took off my jacket and tried to hold it to the wound. He pushed my hands away, his mouth moving wordlessly. His eyes were wide, as if he was seeing something terrifying. Maybe it was the devil extending his blackened hand toward him.

"I'd say I'm sorry, Pops . . ." I shook my head and dropped onto my heels, letting my bloody jacket fall to the ground. "But you're a horrible piece of shit, and you deserve whatever comes to ya, including a bullet. I hope you rot in hell." I rose to my feet and left the building, slamming the metal door behind me.

It was always just me and myself.

Chapter Thirty

Gia

I sat in the backseat of the BMW with my hands folded over my chest and my mind racing. My father glanced back at me in the rearview mirror. I hoped my scowl showcased my discontent.

"Gia," he began, his voice softer.

"No, Dad, don't." I let my head rest against the window. Every bump and pothole made my forehead knock on the glass, and it reminded me of the shitshow I just got re-abducted from.

"Gia, you couldn't stay there. Don't even think about that. He's a Viglione." My father said the name as if it were poison on his tongue. And honestly, it probably was.

"That *Viglione* killed his own father to protect me, and by extension, you as well." I let my face press against the cool window.

"Trust me when I say that he did not kill his father for you." His light eyes glared at me. He was probably right. Enzo never did anything that didn't benefit him in some way. "We're going to have a little chat about that recorder. I'm so disappointed in you." My father's disappointment hurt more than taking a bullet. I grazed my leg where a bullet had once pierced through my flesh and narrowly missed my artery. *That* hurt less than this.

"I know, Daddy," I whispered as I looked at the familiar road which led toward our house. It had been a while since I stepped foot in my own home instead of being kept beneath the wing of the Vigliones. It had only been a couple of weeks, but it felt like forever. He had felt like *home*.

With a sigh, I climbed out of the car and walked toward the front door. Once loved, the beautiful landscaping now seemed ominous. Each flower reached toward the sun, exploding with life. Seeing them made me realize how lifeless I had felt on these grounds.

"Get changed and come to the library," my father said toward me.

I looked down at my torn, muddy jeans. With another sigh, I headed toward my room off the side of the house. We didn't have a fence surrounding the property like Enzo's family, but we had guards posted on the grounds. My father called them our soldiers. They were highly trained young men wishing to crawl up the ranks somehow.

I opened the heavy door and stepped into my bedroom. The air felt stale, so I opened the window. The cool breeze played against my face, teasing my hair. It reminded me of Enzo's touch. I changed out of my jeans and headed toward the library. The socks on my feet made the shining tile floors feel slippery. With a quick inhale, I opened the door and was embraced by the scent of my father's cigars and liquor.

He motioned me inside with a quick gesture, and I went and sat beside him. I crossed my legs and played with my hair nervously, feeling the soft strands against my fingers.

He handed me a glass, and I took a sip of the rich alcohol. It burned my throat on the way down, worming into my empty stomach and emptying heart.

"Giovanna," my father began. Whenever he used my full name, I knew I was in for it. "This was all your idea to get ahead of the Vigliones."

It had all been my idea. My birdbrain plan to eliminate the Vigliones as a rival. Without them in the game, there would be enough peace that I could get out of the business. Leave that all behind without guilt. I felt dead inside from this work, and I just wanted to revive myself again. Being with Enzo had changed my mindset. The business had become more fascinating to me, like it had when I was a child. I enjoyed the nervous excitement in a room full of men that would kill me without a beat of hesitation. To have hands between my legs from a man that would take a bullet for me. There weren't enough men like that in this business anymore. Wandering eyes and roving hands. Enzo only looked at me, and *that* revived me.

"I know, Daddy, but—"

"Then why would you do that? Why would you destroy the chance of taking them down? Where the hell was your loyalty?" He rose to his feet and paced a tight circle. The worst thing anyone in your family could do was call loyalty into question. But realistically, where was it? He wasn't wrong to question it.

"I hardly saw anything. I was pretty much kept as a hostage!" I said with exasperation. I *had* been held hostage, and then one day, I just didn't want to leave.

"You didn't hear them talk about business? Didn't meet anyone they were doing business with?" He raised his eyebrow at me, disbelief clear in his expression.

My lips tightened. "Why do you find that so hard to

believe? Would you have let a rival daughter hang out with you during business hours?"

"Silvio's son would have become lax around you. I know it," he said as he gulped his drink.

"You don't know anything about Enzo!"

"I know enough, Gia. I know he would have wanted you, and you probably would have let him have you." His harsh words were meant to hurt, which was unlike my father. His frustration had coursed through his veins and flown out of his mouth.

"Dad!" I dropped my jaw. "That's a shitty thing to say about your own daughter."

"It's merely an observation. I've seen how you two look at each other. There's something there, and there can't be. Do you hear me?"

"Dad—"

"Do you understand?"

I sat back in the chair and turned away from him. Understanding didn't mean I had to agree. I was a grown woman, after all. The library door clicked shut behind me and drew my attention. Ro walked in and plopped down on the overstuffed chair.

"So we got nothin'?" Ro asked as he leaned forward and put his hands on his knees. I shrugged. "How do we know you didn't tell him about our work? Gia, you can't let dic—"

"Watch yourself," I bit back. "Tread very lightly, little brother. Who I sleep with is none of your business."

"It's our business when you fuck with the only other family that could destroy us," Ro said. "Lying with the goddamn enemy!"

"Jesus Christ, come on. You've had your own share of forbidden romances," I said, making Ro's cheeks flush.

He sat back and crossed his arms over his chest. "Now what?" Ro asked our father.

"We wait and see if they retaliate, which may happen. We got the fucking boss killed. It wasn't our bullet, but our presence is enough to cause a goddamn war."

⌁

Enzo

"This means war," my not-so-little brother said. He pounded his fist on the table.

"Eh, hold on now," I began. Sammy was a carbon copy of Silvio—a big man with an equally large attitude. Marco, my other brother, was on my level—quietly dangerous.

"No, Enzo, goddamn it, get your mind off the broad and pay attention to what has happened! They killed our father!"

I chewed the insides of my cheeks. I couldn't admit it was my gun that killed Silvio. It would mean death for me. But lying could mean death for Gia. In the same breath, the thought of her made my blood run hot, burning my veins. *How dare she? How could she do this to me?* I wasn't always the best toward her, but I had been honest. I was me. She was pretending and lying all along. *Was any of it real?*

A whooshing in my ears, like the initial break of an ocean's wave, drowned out my brothers' voices. My fingers tapped on the table as I thought about Gia. The softness of her face, unshakeable, pretty much only showing emotion when I fucked her. Whenever I fucked her, she felt like an extension of me, a part of my own flesh. Being inside her, making her come on my cock, was a hauntingly incredible memory. I could nearly feel how she squeezed me. How much we trusted each other as I released deep within her. *Goddamn it, Gia.* I ached for her. But also, I *needed* to hate her.

"Enzo?" My brother's voice rang out, but it sounded so far away. I was drowning in the current of my memory. The tide pulled me under. "Enzo!" His harshness snapped me back into the moment, placing my feet on dry land.

"What?" I looked at them, my eyes darting from one to the other.

"Did you listen to a word we said?"

"Sammy, I have a lot on my mind right now," I snapped. Even aside from Gia, I had a lot on my mind. With Silvio gone, I was next in line. I would have to take over the jobs I never agreed with in the first place. I had to handle the colossal mistakes and fuck-ups of my father and his father before him. But I would not run this family with Silvio's heavy hand. If I had a son, I wouldn't torment and abuse him and use him to fulfill voyeuristic fantasies. Silvio did everything he did under the guise of making a man out of me, but that wasn't what it was about. He cared about control and molding me into what *he* wanted me to be.

"You're being a puss—" Marco began.

I interrupted him by standing and slamming my fist on the table. The sound echoed through the large kitchen. "Enough! Both of you! We can talk about this later, but right now, I have a lot of shit to figure out!" I turned and left the kitchen, refusing to give them the opportunity to grace me with even one more word.

I walked through the empty halls toward my bedroom. My heart ached from the loss of Gia, though I could never trust her again. She betrayed me. Not only that, she put my family in danger. *She* was the reason Silvio was dead. *Fucking bitch.*

That yo-yo of emotions was getting to my head. When I inhaled, I longed for her. When I exhaled, I despised her. *She probably handed the recording off to her parents, fully loaded ammunition for them to use against us.* She saw and heard so much. *I never should have brought her along. I knew better. She wasn't one of us. I forgot she was a lioness, not a sweet little house cat.* Gia growled, not purred. She would hunt before she ever became the hunted. She was stronger than me in some ways, which made her that much more dangerous.

Once in my room, Atheist leapt from his bed, limping slightly as he walked toward me. He pushed his body against my leg and shook his mighty head. Stitches poked from the shaved skin in his armpit. That was another matter to deal with, but it would have to wait. For now, I was just glad to see his big, stupid face back at home.

With a sigh, I slipped off my shoes and sat on the couch, my body heavy and tired. I looked around the room, at reminders of Gia's presence. Her oversized t-shirt on my bed, her brush on the nightstand, and her bag on the floor. *Her bag!* I stood and grabbed the bag off the floor, lifting it onto the bed. I rifled through the main compartment, pulling out clothing and girly shit. Powder from her makeup bag shook onto my bed as I turned it upside down and emptied. *Damn it,* I thought as I tried to wipe it off my comforter, smearing it and staining the white fabric. Just another reminder of Gia etched into my life.

I threw the bag onto the bed and groaned, knowing she'd taken whatever recorder she had with her. She was going to destroy my life. *Fucking Gia!*

Out of the corner of my eye, I saw a little zipper on the

front of the bag. There was a small tent in the fabric, hardly noticeable unless you were looking for it. I grabbed the bag and opened the zipper, feeling around with my fingers. The pocket was so small that my hand couldn't fit inside it. I gripped something and pulled it out. It was a dismantled and destroyed recorder. At least, what used to be a recorder. It was smashed to bits. My heart sank at the sight of it, knowing Gia had told the truth. I should have checked her stuff before I let the rage boil through my veins. *Does it change anything, though? Really?* I threw the recorder onto the ground, and it skipped across the carpet. *Gia still came into my home under false pretenses. She cozied up to me for intel, and I'll never trust her again.* Fractured webbing stretched across the surface of my heart. The thought of never knowing how she really felt about me made me sick to my stomach. How much I poured onto her and inside her. *Was any of it real?*

Chapter Thirty-One

Gia

The soft rumble of a car driving away caught my attention, and I ran toward the window. I couldn't see anything, but I could feel . . . something. Ever since we left the docks, I felt watched. *You're being paranoid,* I thought to myself.

I stood, slipped on my flip-flops, and walked toward the main house. The pictures of my smiling family dotting the hallway almost nauseated me in comparison to the dreary pictures of Enzo's family. No one looked happy there, not under Silvio. *Silvio,* I thought, remembering the gunshot and having to run. I had to leave Enzo behind to deal with the mess I created. It was my family who shot first, forcing him to shoot last.

Is he okay?

I knew Enzo would never forgive me, and that made my heart bleed. I felt the warm remnants of my soul dripping into my stomach. Enzo was the first person I'd felt feelings for in a very long time—my whole life, perhaps. Before him,

I thought I was a cold, emotionless being, incapable of feeling. Enzo woke up those emotions inside me, making me feel alive.

I knocked before walking into the library. The heavy conversation halted the moment they saw me. I was a traitor to not only his family, but my own.

"Don't stop on my account." I rolled my hand in a gesture to carry on and wrapped myself in a blanket draped over the chair as I sat and curled into myself.

"Gia," Ro said sternly. "We need time."

"Time? For what?" My gaze snapped to him, my lip trembling.

Ro wiped his forehead. "To trust you again," he said with a quiver to his words.

Trust me? A sharp pain stabbed through my chest. His accusation wasn't unfounded, but it still hurt. I'd spent my entire life being faithful to this family, even as it took everything from me. I never even dated because I felt married to the family business.

"Ro, you have to understand why—"

"No, Gia, I don't. I'll never understand why. You *hated* their family as much as we do. The Vigliones made you sick! You were willing to bring them down, and we had a prime opportunity to do so. All of it was for nothing! Was getting fucked by the son of Silvio fucking Viglione worth it?" He looked at me with a curl of his lip.

He was laying the shame on thick, trying to make me feel guilty. *Do I?* I began to question everything, whether what happened was merely a terrible dream. It wasn't, it couldn't have been, right? Yes, I could still remember the horrible things Lorenzo tried to do to me, the way Enzo protected me. His firm yet now familiar touch. If I closed my eyes long enough, I could see his face etched to perfection in my mind's eye. No, it wasn't a dream. But I might have dreamed how I thought Enzo felt about me. He loved to fuck me, and I thoroughly enjoyed him fucking me, but was there anything more for him? Was I merely a trophy for his wall, a rival notch on his bedpost? I needed to let these memories of him go. It was fun-ish while it lasted.

"Hello?" Ro interrupted my thoughts, snapping his fingers in front of my face. "Did you hear me?"

"Yes, I heard you. I'm a piece of shit. I know that, okay?" I could already feel myself beginning to wither away, suffocating on the air of tension within this house.

Enzo

I WALKED into the club and reached over the counter to grab a beer. The stool squeaked when I sat.

"Where's your broad?" the men asked in unison before laughing.

I flashed them a tight-lipped glare, making the laughter die as quickly as it had begun.

"Don't worry, your brothers will take care of her." Bullseye dropped his hand of cards to the table, spreading them like a fan. "Full house."

"Ah, fuck. You got cards up your sleeves?" Kenny asked as he threw his cards down and pushed the pile of chips toward Bullseye.

With a quick shake of his sleeves, he showed he had no hidden cards, that it was all just his luck. I kept my gaze straight ahead as I played with the cap of my beer, twirling it around my fingers.

The weight of Bullseye's words hit me much too late. The conversation had long been left behind. "Wait, what did you mean, Bullseye?"

"What? That I had a full house? Aces and threes."

"No, idiot, about my brothers," I said as I rubbed between my eyes.

"Your brothers will take care of her, that's all I said." Bullseye stacked the cards and began to shuffle them.

"I know that's what you said, but *why* did you say that?" I sat taller.

"It's nothing, Enzo, relax. Nothing to worry your pretty little head about." Bullseye chuckled.

I stood, my heart racing, and drew my revolver. I cocked it and placed it to the side of his head. The other men dropped their cards and let their hands rest on their hips.

"What do you know?" I asked again, pressing the barrel against his temple.

Bullseye rolled his eyes and grabbed the barrel, pushing it toward the ground. "You ain't gonna shoot me, Enzo, so put the gun down," Bullseye said with humorless laughter. He was right. I couldn't shoot him. He was a made man. "Your brothers have been keeping an eye on that Silvani bitch, is all."

A shiver crawled up my spine and stopped in my throat. I swallowed hard. "You didn't think to fucking tell me that?" I knew why my brothers were watching her. My cheeks flushed with warmth.

"I didn't think it was a big deal. One less Silvani to deal with," Bullseye said with a shrug as he drew his cigar to his lips and let it hang from them. "Deal up," he said through clenched teeth, cradling the cigar between his jaws.

Realization washed over me. I hated Gia for doing what she'd done to me, but I couldn't let her die for what happened at my hands. It was *my* smoking gun, not hers or her father's. What a time to gain a fucking conscience.

Without another word, I left the club and headed toward the parking lot. I heard them call to me from behind, but there was nothing more to talk about today. I had only one thing on my mind.

Thoughts jumbled in my head. The path I took was unmemorable, and I didn't recall the twisting turns it took to get back home. I pulled into the big garage and hit the button to close the door. Water dripped from the ceiling, splattering and spreading across the concrete.

My steps echoed as I ran up the stairs and made my way to my room. I opened the door to my bedroom and inhaled the remaining scent of Gia. I ducked beneath my bed, pulled out a lockbox, and opened it, rustling through the paperwork. My hand grabbed a huge stack of money crisply banded together. I fanned it through my fingers, grabbed some of the paperwork, and put it in her bag. With a quick swivel of my head I went to the closet and grabbed some clothes, stuffing them over the money and papers.

"Come on, Atheist, let's go for a ride," I said. He didn't need to be told twice. He bounded toward the door, wagging his nubby tail. His limp was all but gone, and he was always ready for a car ride. Atheist looked back at me and whined. I grabbed his leash, and we walked down the long hallway, his nails clicking on the marble floors. I opened the car door and let him hop into the backseat. "I wish I was half as excited about life as you are, boy," I whispered as I sat in the driver's seat, his big, blocky head beside mine.

Nighttime blanketed the sky as I headed toward the mansion on the hill. I knew her family had guards on the property, but it didn't deter me. I could outmaneuver any of those goons with my gun. Atheist's body tensed as we pulled around the back of the property on a narrow gravel road that wasn't meant for cars. He sensed the anxiety racing through me even though I tried to keep it hidden.

"Stay here, boy. I'll be right back." I rubbed his head. "Hopefully."

Crickets chirped as I walked along the wood line. Mosquitoes buzzed around my head, their annoying sounds vibrating in my ears. A beam of light broke through the darkness, and I pinned myself against a tree, holding my breath in anticipation.

"Yeah, no, I miss you too, babe. Tell me what you're wearing." The voice of a young guard penetrated the silence. I rolled my eyes at his callous disregard for his job. If I could skirt him easily, so could my brothers. "Yeah? That's it? Tell me more." The guard's voice retreated with his footsteps.

I ducked as I walked along the shrubs that lined the walkway toward the side of the house. Like me, Gia lived in the extension of the home, meant for whoever would super-sede their father.

I flattened myself against the side of the house and ducked as far as I could as a beam of light swept across the yard in front of me. *Fuck,* I thought as I withdrew my revolver and clutched it at my side. The beam did one more pass before disappearing.

When the night air was silent and dark again, I peered through her window and watched her walk into the bedroom from her bathroom. Her hair was thrown into a messy bun on her head, and loose hairs fell from it and framed her face. She wore a cami, the thin straps falling past her bare shoulders. Even from here, I saw the mounds of her breasts beneath the thin fabric, and blood rushed from my extremities straight for my cock. *Not now!* I tried to tell myself. Seeing her made me hungry for her, even if I fucking hated her. The same hunger I had for her before she finally started to satiate my cravings. A colder desire that stemmed from my cock.

I holstered my revolver and went for the doorknob. I twisted it, expecting it to be locked, but it wasn't. Gia made a move to scream, but I raced in and wrapped my hand around her mouth. "Shut up, Gia, it's me."

She mumbled through my grasp, and I smirked because I knew she was cursing me. Gia would always be unapologetically herself. I kicked the door closed, slowly moved my hand away, and caught the tail end of her angry words.

"Goddamn you!" She wiped at her mouth. "What are you doing here?"

"My brothers want you dead. They've been casing this place," I said, sitting beside her on the bed.

"The guards—"

I gestured toward myself. "Hello, hi, those guards didn't do much of shit."

"Well, fuck. Why? What would they want me—" Her eyes widened. "You didn't . . ."

I dropped my gaze for a moment before meeting hers again. "I didn't say you guys did it. I just didn't correct them. I didn't know what else to do. I couldn't say I did it."

"Yeah, you couldn't possibly do that. Putting a bounty on my head seems like a much more reasonable choice." She sucked her teeth as she looked away from me.

"I still think you're a backstabbing whore," I told her callously.

She gasped, threw her hand up, and smacked me. The blow was well deserved.

"Fuck you, Enzo," she hissed.

"Come on." I stood and gestured toward her.

She shook her head. "I'm not going anywhere with you!"

"You can come willingly, Giovanna, or I will take you by force. Your choice," I said calmly, placing a hand on my revolver.

"Fuck off. If you try to force me, I'll yell for the guards."

"If you yell for them, their deaths will be on you."

I grabbed her arm, and she tightened her lips as she stared at me, shooting daggers from her beautiful eyes. I didn't care how mad she was at me, as long as she was alive.

"What about my family?" Gia asked as she shrugged out of my grasp to grab some clothes.

"They don't want your family, Gia. They want you. Now hurry the fuck up!"

"Are we going back to your house?" she asked, stuffing her clothes into a bag.

"No, we aren't," I said, hiding the sadness from her. My house could never be my home again. Nothing would be the same after what I planned to do.

"You left Atheist?" she asked with raised eyebrows.

"Fuck no, I ain't leaving that dog nowhere. He's in the car, waiting for *us*."

"Fine, let's go," Gia said flatly. She looked back at her room one last time.

Nothing would be the same after this.

Chapter Thirty-Two

Gia

I adjusted my position in the passenger seat. We'd been driving for four hours—in a cramped luxury car, no less. My legs were numb and achy. Worse, Atheist kept hopping onto my lap and hanging his head out the window. His silly expression as his tongue lolled out of his mouth was why I kept allowing it. "Where the hell are we going?"

"Out of the vicinity of the fucking city," Enzo said.

"Are we literally running away right now?" I groaned as the morning sun attacked my eyes through the windshield. I lowered the visor and looked away from it.

"We aren't running away. I'm making a conscious decision to get us the fuck out of there right now, okay? Will you stop questioning me?" he said as he snatched down his visor. "You act like I want to be taking you anywhere."

"Enzo— "

His words overflowed and spilled past his lips. "You betrayed me, Gia. You came into my house and bed. You made me trust you, and it was all based on lies. Was *any* of this real? I let you into my life, I let you into my h—" He banged a fist on the steering wheel. "No, you know what? Fuck this." He stopped speaking, as if he was trying to keep himself from exploding. I deserved it.

I sat silently, with my gaze on the mile markers as they blazed by us. "I'm sorry," I said with a deflated breath. "You don't understand . . ."

"Of course I fucking do. I understand about family and business, I get that. But you didn't need to get so cozy with me. Business is fucking business."

"I'm sorry I hurt you."

"What is it you always say? Such is this life? Such is this fucking life." Enzo hit the steering wheel again.

"Why are you the only one who can be hurt? You've wanted me since I was carried into your fucking house. How do I know if any of this was real for you? How do I know you felt anything more for me than lust? You pretty much ra—"

"Think carefully before you speak, Gia. Tread very lightly."

I crossed my arms over my chest and turned away from him.

"Guess we're back to square one," he said with a sigh.

We drove in silence for what felt like an eternity before Enzo took a right turn up a driveway. My eyes crawled along the landscape, landing on the well-kept colonial on top of a hill overlooking the woods. It made my jaw drop.

"Where are we?" I asked with wonder in my eyes.

"My safe house."

"You have your own fucking safe house?" My jaw remained slack.

"Yeah, our family does a little more dangerous shit than

yours," he said. He leaned toward my chest, talking into my boobs. "Can you hear all that?"

I rolled my eyes and pushed him away. "You're being childish."

He parked the car and let Atheist out of the back seat. The dog took off along the rolling hills, looking like a little black bear the farther he ran. Massive trees surrounded us on all four sides and made me feel tiny in comparison. We *were* tiny in comparison. Nestled within the woods was the house, buried behind the wall of trees. It truly was perfect.

"When were you here last?" I asked as he opened the big white door. The air felt stale inside, as if it had been empty for quite some time. The room welcomed the light of the open door, and I walked to the curtains and opened them, letting in more of it. Dust coated my hands, and I wiped it on my pants. The sunbeams streamed through the window, creating a rainbow of color on the tan hardwood floors.

"Last year? I think," he said as he dropped our bags by the door. I looked back at him, and he brushed a hand through his dark hair.

I cocked an eyebrow. "Why were you here?"

"Not that I should tell you shit, but do you remember the Romano case?"

"The butchered double murder . . ." I gasped. "You?" Him? The Enzo I know wouldn't have been so careless, leaving pieces of himself behind."

"Not my best work. I got a little sloppy and had to lay low for a while."

I furrowed my brow at him. "No one knows this is here?"

Enzo shook his head. "Not even Silvio knew about this house."

I looked around the home. Aside from the thin dust coating some things, it was meticulous. The leather furniture wrapped around the room and faced a large television. I spotted the corner of a pool table in the middle room, and it sent a flood of memories through my mind.

The cold wood of the table against my bare skin.

"How do you keep anyone from finding this?"

"Fake everything." A smirk crept onto his lips, as if he were proud of himself. He should have been. This was an accomplishment. To get a fucking house as a ghost was impressive.

I sat on the couch with a huff and stretched my legs. Atheist bounded into the open door and hopped onto the couch with muddy paws. "Oh, come on, Atheist!" I yelled as I tried to stop him from stepping on my clothes, but his wiggling body seemed more determined to leap onto my lap the harder I fought him off.

Enzo called to him, and he hopped off the couch and ran to his side, sitting obediently at his feet. His body still wiggled with excitement.

"You can have the room at the end of the hall. It's got its own bathroom." He gestured toward the door at the end of the long hallway. The walls were void of pictures or any signs of life. Not only was Enzo a ghost, so was the home. I found myself enjoying the serenity of the emptiness—a clean slate of memories.

I could get used to this.

I lifted my bag and headed toward the room. I opened the flimsy wooden door, and it squeaked on its hinges. The room seemed staged, like a house made up for a showing. Was it made up when he bought it? Did he even change a thing? A crisp purple-and-white paisley quilt lay on top of the large bed, tucked in on three of its sides. The side closest to the headboard was neatly folded over itself. I rubbed my hand along the glossy surface of the rich reddish-brown mahogany dresser.

"I'll be back!" Enzo called from the living room. "I'm gonna go get groceries and shit."

I didn't call back to him. I just flopped onto the soft memory foam bed and let it absorb me into its center. Atheist ran in and looked at me, his tail wagging.

"No! Stay!"

He crouched down, his butt in the air.

"No, Atheist! It's a white fucking bed!"

Atheist hesitated for only a moment before leaping onto the bed and leaving big brown footprints on the crisp white blanket. He had completely forgotten the injury he'd received not long ago, but the hair was still shorter in that area of his armpit.

"Your dad's going to be mad!" I laughed as I patted his head. Why did a thing as simple as a dog muddying a blanket feel so *normal* to me? Like I had been missing out on such normalcy. Maybe I had been.

Goddamn it, Enzo.

Chapter Thirty-Three

Enzo

My focus kept wandering to Gia's eyes every so often, but she kept her gaze ahead, staring at the TV. I lay sprawled across the couch, my leg hanging off the edge. Atheist was nestled beneath it with his body pressed against my calf. Gia dropped her head into her hand as she leaned back in the recliner.

A knock on the door made me jump, and Atheist struggled from beneath my leg as he scurried to his feet. He released a guttural bark, looking back at me with tensed muscles. Gia sat up tall, her eyebrows furrowed.

"I thought you said no one knows about this place?" Gia asked.

"They don't," I said as I stood. Beside the door, I drew my revolver, calling to whoever waited on the other side. "Who is it?" I asked as I cocked the gun's hammer. My heart raced at the thought of any other human gracing my doorstep with their presence. No one else was welcome here.

"It's me," a low, familiar voice said.

I opened the door and saw Bullseye standing on my doorstep, his bulky frame leaving a large shadow on the ground behind him. He pushed himself inside, turning on his heels once he saw Gia sitting on the chair.

"What the fuck is she doing here?" Bullseye asked with deserved harshness.

"What do you want, Bullseye?" I holstered my revolver but kept my hand wrapped around the grip. "How did you even know I was here?"

Bullseye waved his phone in my face, showing a GPS ping on the screen. "I was going to tell you that the Silvani bitch is missing. I was hoping your brothers took care of her, but to my surprise, here she is."

"That's none of your business. *She* is not your business," I said with a harsh gesture toward her.

"She killed your fucking father, Enzo." With a swift motion, he racked his pistol, raised it, and aimed it toward Gia.

She didn't even react, facing death so stoically. Instead of yelling or begging, she merely flashed her dark eyes at him.

"No!" I screamed as my heart thumped against my chest. A gunshot rang out, causing the windows to rattle. The sound ricocheted off the walls, and my eyes clenched as the loud crack of gunfire caused a moment of dizzying confusion.

"Enzo!"

Bullseye's body slumped forward, his knees hitting the ground first, followed by the rest of his body. The thud made the glasses on the table rattle. The big silver pistol dropped to the ground beside his right hand. I looked up at Gia, her hand cupped over her mouth, stifling her sounds.

"Goddamn it," I said with a sigh.

Bullseye was one of my closest friends. He was pretty much family. I'd grown up with him by Silvio's side, and he became a made man in front of me, an honor to witness. At that moment, I had to choose between a made man—knowing his worth in our circle was so high that everyone would turn on me—or my girl.

Fuck, she isn't even my girl! I rubbed the bridge of my nose. *I chose someone who broke my heart.*

"This is not good, Enzo." Gia stood, her hand still firmly held up to her mouth. "You just killed a made man."

My stare lurched toward Gia, my lips drawn tight. "I know what I fucking did," I said. My stomach churned with nervous energy. My head would be on a fucking platter if I showed my face around home. "This is all your fault! None of this would have happened! None of it. Silvio? Bullseye? All because ya wanted to climb to the fucking top."

Gia's lip quivered as she stared at me with a gaze that almost made me drop mine. "I never wanted to climb to the top of nothing! I was promised a sum of money if I—"

"So you did it for money? That makes it better?" My eyes narrowed on her. I stepped aside as blood flowed in a thick line toward my shoes.

"Oh, fuck off. Everything you do is for money!"

"For fuck's sake." I shook my head.

"I wanted money to get *out* of this business. I didn't want to climb anywhere but away. I'm done with this lifestyle." She sat with a deflated drop in her shoulders.

My resolve softened. "You can't just get out of this business. You know that."

"I had to try! Nothing but pain has come from this life. Disgusting men have raped me more times than I can count. There's been so much death and destruction. I'm sick of having to commit murder just to see the light of the next day. I'm just tired." Her eyelashes fluttered as she fought back tears.

"Come here," I commanded, but she shook her head and remained planted in her seat. "Gia!" I gave her a moment to comply, but she continued to ignore me. I walked toward her, grabbed a fistful of her hair, and dragged her across the room. I stopped beside Bullseye's body, throwing her in front of his lifeless eyes. She struggled against my grasp. "This is why you can never escape the business! There is no getting lax, no peace, nothing but wondering if your next mistake will finally be a fatal one." She whimpered against my grasp, the artery in her neck throbbing. "I just killed an un-fucking-touchable man, the greatest shot on the East Coast, for *you*."

She grasped the wrist of the hand holding her hair. "Enzo—"

"We are in this fucking business now . . . together. There ain't no going back from this. This is it." I gestured toward the body in front of us. "I don't wanna be stuck in this fucking home with someone I hate." I raised her to her feet by her hair.

Her lip trembled and her eyes glossed over. "You don't hate me," she whispered.

I growled against her neck and tossed her away from me. She stumbled and looked back at me with eyebrows raised.

"You don't get to say how I feel, Gia. You lost that privilege the moment you betrayed me." I grabbed Bullseye's arms. Blood had soaked through his white dress shirt and tie-dyed it red. "Help me get rid of him."

Nothing would be the same after that.

Chapter Thirty-Four

Gia

By the time we got rid of Bullseye's body, a curtain of darkness surrounded us. Crickets chirped with a beautiful sound I didn't normally hear in the city. Atheist trotted beside me, shaking the lake water off his coat. Enzo sighed behind me.

"What are we going to do?" I asked without looking back at him.

"There's nothing we can do. It's done."

"Should we leave?"

He stopped, his voice projecting when he spoke. "There isn't anywhere to go. We don't have the money to just fucking move." His hands began to gesture, showing how Italian he really was. "This is what we got for now, so make the best outta it."

The best out of it? I shook my head. *Fat chance.* I was wanted by at least two families: the Vigliones *and* the Silvanis. I was also associated with the man who killed Bullseye, turning the eyes of several other families on me as well.

"Did you toss his phone in the water?" I asked.

"No, I gotta know if he told anyone about us," Enzo said as he grabbed the black cell phone from his back pocket.

"Well, destroy it when you're done with it," I said. This situation felt hopeless, and I just wanted to go back to my room. *I'm sick of getting rid of bodies. I'm tired of throwing a piece of myself in with them.*

I walked into the house that felt less and less like home all of a sudden. Now it reminded me of the business that I was trying to escape from in the first place. Maybe Bullseye had taken my sense of peace when he took his last breath.

The door slammed behind me, startling me. I turned back toward Enzo and shook my head. "I want to go home."

"This is your home now, *babygirl*," he said with ice on his tongue. The way he called me "babygirl" wasn't how he used to say it, and now it almost felt like a mockery.

"I didn't kill Bullseye, and I don't want to be involved with someone who did." My gaze dropped to the bloodstain on the floor.

"Hate to tell you, but you already are." He rushed past me to go toward his room.

"You can't hold me here!" I yelled, halting him.

He turned on his heels, coming back to face me. The intensity in his eyes stabbed through me. He brushed the hair from my face, still matted and sticky. "Here's the thing. I hate you right now, but you're mine, Giovanna. Give me a little time and I'll remind you of that."

His hot, gravelly words burned through my chest, and my breath caught in my throat as they burrowed into me.

"I'm not yours," I snarled. He made that very clear to me before now.

"Go to my room," he commanded, pointing down the hall.

"I'm going to take a shower. I'm covered in blood and dirt," I said as I tugged at my stained clothing.

"You're gonna be covered in something else." He gestured again, more firmly. "Go!"

I knew what he wanted. Whenever he was stressed or frustrated, he wanted to bury those feelings inside me. Did I want it? Yes. Did I want him to just go fuck himself instead? Also yes.

I followed him to the bedroom, staying steps behind him as I contemplated what to do and whether I was willing to give my body to him again. He didn't fucking deserve it, but neither did I. He led me to his bathroom and leaned against the counter.

"Get in the shower," he said with a husky voice that gave me no room to argue. Though I'd still try. He brushed a muddy hand through his hair.

"I'm not getting naked in front of you like this." I cocked my hip and rested my hand on it.

Without dropping his gaze, he began to unbutton his dress shirt, the muscles rippling beneath the taut skin of his stomach. The edge of a tattoo peeked from his side. My mouth unintentionally fell open and stayed that way. His fierce blue eyes remained trained on me as he unholstered his revolver and let his pants fall to the ground. There he stood in front of me, his erection painfully obvious through his boxers. I saw the contours of his head, thick and throbbing, through the thin fabric.

"Get undressed. I won't ask again." He placed the revolver on the marble countertop, his hand hovering over it.

I shook my head, backing up until I met the wall. He grabbed his gun, cocked it, and walked toward me to confront my refusal. He pressed the barrel against my head, the cool metal giving me goosebumps. I shivered down to my very core. It should have scared me, but it excited me. My life was in his hand, and a slight movement of his finger could end it.

I had no choice but to trust him. I looked up at him and took in a sharp breath.

He pressed the barrel into my skin. "Giovanna." He said my name in a harsh way that forced me to listen.

I bit my lip as I grabbed the bottom of my shirt, shrugging away from him as I lifted it over my head. He growled when he saw I wasn't wearing a bra and lowered the barrel, letting it run slowly between my breasts.

"Fuck, babygirl," he said before kissing me with a roughness that felt familiar. Full of hatred and lust.

That was how he used to call me babygirl.

He dipped the barrel into my waistband and gripped my ass roughly with his free hand before pulling my pants down my thighs. Enzo rubbed the gun between my legs, against the silk of my soaked panties.

"I need these off," he commanded, the gun rubbing back and forth between my thighs. I slid my pants off the rest of the way. "Good girl," he whispered.

With a movement of his thumb, he uncocked the revolver and set it on the counter. His fingers hooked into the sides of my panties, pulling them down with hunger in his eyes. His lips found mine for a quick moment while he pulled his boxers down, leaving me wanting more. He stood in front of me, so hard that it made me weak. With a hand wrapped around himself, he tipped his chin toward the shower.

Steam billowed up and fogged the mirror when I turned on the shower. I stepped beneath the water, closed the glass door, and let the heat wash my sins away. The brown and red remnants swirled around the drain. With my eyes still shut, I heard the door open and close. Enzo stepped in front of me. I looked at him, watching water droplets fall onto him and roll off his defined cheekbones. He brushed my hair back and fisted a handful of it.

"Are you going to fuck me?" I asked with a nervous bite of my lip.

"Nah," he said with a sadistic smile. "I prefer to just fuck with ya."

My stomach tightened. "Are we really back to this?"

"I don't trust you, Giovanna." Despite the warmth surrounding us, his words held an icy edge. "And honestly, you don't deserve it."

Maybe he was right, but it didn't sting any less. With an annoyed snap in every motion, I grabbed the shampoo and washed my hair, ignoring him and his fierce stare. My cheeks flushed with heat as my eyes wandered to where he stroked himself. "You aren't being fair. I can't touch my—"

Enzo pinned me to the wall. His hand dropped and palmed my pussy. "You can't touch yourself because I'll be the only one making you come," he said with a smirk.

I can play this game, too, motherfucker.

We finished letting the tales of tonight wash away and stepped out of the shower. Enzo tossed a towel at me. He was excited the entire time, and he had to be getting sick of it. I'd never quite wanted something as badly as I did right then, and I physically ached for him.

"You really aren't going to fuck me?" I asked as he started to put on a fresh pair of boxers.

He looked up at me as he balanced on one leg, a grin creeping across his face. "Nope." He pulled up the boxers, which only highlighted his erection.

Come the fuck on!

He stepped closer and grazed my chin with a forefinger. "I'll fuck you when I'm good and ready. When *I* want it, not you. Though, if you want, you can suck my dick." He cocked an eyebrow and touched himself.

I looked at him with a heated expression. Of course I wanted to suck his dick, but not when he played fucking mind games.

"Fuck you, Enzo," I snapped before turning to leave his room.

He grabbed my arm, pulling me backward. "I know what you'll do the moment you get in there."

"And?" I sucked my teeth.

"You can sleep in here with me tonight," he said with a half-cocked smile.

"No. I'm not your prisoner." I shrugged out of his grasp.

"I told you. Once I remind you what I can do to your body, you won't feel like one." He lifted his eyebrows. "Come to bed."

With a huff, I turned to leave.

"Eh, where you going?"

"To get pajamas, you dick," I said before leaving the room.

I hated to love that piece of shit.

Chapter Thirty-Five

Enzo

I woke up to Gia lying within my arms. It felt incredible and familiar, and for a moment, I forgot the situation we were in. I picked up Bullseye's phone and guessed his password very quickly—his son's birthday. With a thorough search of his phone, I learned he'd made no outbound calls or sent any texts in the time it would have taken him to get here. His last texts were to his family, and they made my stomach twist. Everyone expected *the* Bullseye to make it home, and soon it would become obvious he wouldn't.

I set down the phone and looked at Gia. Her chest rose and fell rhythmically, and her lips formed a slight pout. Did I want to fuck her? Abso-fucking-lutely. But I wanted to play with her mind more. I needed her to crave me so badly that she would dream about my cock all over again. Just the thought of her needing me made me swell again. After an entire evening of waxing and waning excitement, it was becoming a physical ache.

Goddamn it, Gia.

How easy would it be to give in to her? To slide deep within her like she begged for? I wiped my hand through my hair before climbing out of bed and spreading the curtains. The sun blared through the glass, sending its bright rays across the hardwood floors. Gia stirred, groaning as she turned away and pulled the blanket over her head. I despised the way my heart raced at the mere sight of her. No woman had ever made me feel the way she did when I was in bed with her. Shit, even outside of the bed. She kept me on my toes, her aggression and confidence an incredible complement to her beauty. I never knew if she'd try to kill me or fuck me. Some days I was fine with either.

"You really won't fuck me?" she asked from beneath the dark quilt.

I smirked. "Nah," I said with a calmness that contradicted the racing pulse in my cock.

"You're a piece of shit."

"Yeah, yeah, I know." I shrugged my shoulders. "Come on, wake up." I walked over and ripped the blanket down.

She looked back at me with an exaggerated sigh. "Why?"

She reached for the blanket, but I pulled it away from her. The fleece had shielded the soft curve of her ass peeking just beneath her t-shirt, her black panties trying to cover what I'd thought about all night. Seeing her like that nearly put me over the edge. I wanted to rip into her and tear her apart. A low growl vibrated my throat as she arched her back with purpose and sat up, wiping her tired eyes.

"We need to get rid of Bullseye's car," I said, slapping her thigh. "Come on, get up."

"Why the fuck do I have to go?" she whined.

"Because, while I'm ninety-five percent sure Bullseye

didn't tell anyone my whereabouts, I sure as fuck ain't gonna leave that remaining five to chance."

"I can handle myself." Her fierce stare bored into me. I knew she could, but still.

"I ain't risking it. Come the fuck on, Gia!" I commanded, my patience wearing thin.

She rolled over, turning her back to me like a defiant child. She arched her back, exposing more of the thin black fabric between her legs. I rolled my eyes because I knew exactly what she was trying to do. She'd entered herself into the game as a contender, and she would be a formidable foe.

I shook my head before I clambered onto the bed and pressed myself against her ass. I got hard before I even touched the heat of her skin. She writhed beneath me, and I leaned over and pinned her against the bed. She let a soft moan escape her full lips, and I cocked my eyebrow.

"Gia, I'm not playing with you. We have to go. My guy is waiting for me at his shop." As much as I would have loved to rip those panties down and take her right then, we had to get the car to the shop before it opened. Not one to miss an opportunity, I ran my hands roughly over the back of her neck and down every curve. My palm grazed her ass and I smacked it, leaving a red imprint. "Come on."

"Fine," she said with a pout as she sat up.

"You're so fucking difficult," I said as I climbed off the bed and went to get dressed.

Gia

"Do you even trust this guy?" I asked as he drove Bullseye's SUV away from the house.

"I've known him since I was a kid, yeah," he said as his eyes darted on the road in front of him.

"Didn't you also know Bullseye since you were a kid?" I crossed my arms and looked at the scenery moving past the window.

"Bullseye was more Silvio's friend than mine."

The car slowed before making a left-hand turn into the parking lot of a huge garage. The building towered over us and spread across the length of the property. Cars of various types dotted the asphalt, some with license plates and others without. I craned my head to look at the bright blue-and-yellow building. Enzo pulled up to a heavy-duty garage door over one of the bays and drove over a cable on the ground. After a moment of silence, the door opened with a mechanical whirr, and a man in a grease-covered t-shirt and jeans motioned us inside.

Enzo drove into the stagnant air of the garage. It smelled like grease, oil, and gasoline. He climbed out of the car.

"Jameson." Enzo nodded toward the man.

"What we got here?" Jameson asked, his voice so deep and alluring it caught my attention.

I stepped out of the car, putting my feet onto the dark stains on the cracked concrete. When I turned to look back at Jameson, his eyebrows lifted.

"More importantly, who is this?" he asked with a butter-smooth voice that made Enzo tense.

"Don't bother. She's a Silvani." Enzo's voice was intentionally harsh.

"No shit. Daughter of Sylvester?" Jameson stepped

toward me and reached for my hand, bringing it to his lips. "What a *pleasure.*"

His words and seductive tone made heat rise into my chest and cheeks. He brushed a greasy hand through his light blond hair. Enzo's posture stiffened and he dropped a hand instinctively to his revolver. Jameson was oblivious to Enzo's actions. His green eyes locked on me, and a handsome smile crept across his face.

"Jameson," Enzo snapped, making the man turn toward him again. "Ya know what I need, right?"

"Not particularly. I keep phone calls brief for a reason."

"I need a full wipe and tear down. I want every piece fucking stripped and sold. Spread the parts as far as you can."

"Whose car is it, Enzo?"

"You know better than to ask me that." Enzo shook his head. "The less you know, the better."

"You act like I ain't gonna run the plates. I'm giving you the chance to explain."

"Bianchi," Enzo said in a harsh whisper.

"Bullseye? *The* Bullseye?" Jameson's eyes widened. "How? Why?"

"He was going to kill Gia." Enzo gestured toward me.

Jameson shot a glance at me, his eyes moving over my curves. He nodded as if he understood why a man would kill for me. I couldn't understand, though, because I didn't deserve to live more than Bullseye. He was the one who'd been faithful to Enzo, not me.

"Well, you got yourself in quite the situation, my friend," Jameson said with a rise in his tone that made me tense.

"I know, Jameson, just help me get outta it, will ya?"

"After what you did for my family, you know I will, but

you know the saying about playing stupid games and what you win, right?"

"Yeah, yeah, I know. What was I supposed to do? Let him kill her?"

Jameson's eyes shot to me again, his stare tunneling through me, making a smile cross my lips that was aimed at Enzo. "Guess not," he said as a sly smirk crossed his lips.

Chapter Thirty-Six

Enzo

I ushered Gia into the house and slammed the door behind me. She kept her eyes on mine, squinting at me.

"What?" I snapped.

Her gaze was steadfast. "What the fuck is your problem?" she asked with a curious cock of her head. As if she didn't know.

"Nothing, Gia." My voice was precisely as harsh as it needed to be.

She reached out and grabbed my arm when I tried to walk away. "What the hell, Enzo?"

I spun on my heels and threw her against the wall, making it quake behind her. Her mouth fell open, her eyes narrowing once more. "I saw how ya were looking at Jameson. How he looked at you."

"I contemplated asking for his number on the way back here." A sadistic grin painted her face, her eyes fiery.

"You're a fucking whore. I don't know why I thought you'd be any different."

"You haven't thought shit about me. You hate me, and frankly, I'm not a fan of you, either."

"That's not what you were saying last night . . . this morning . . . You were begging me to fuck you. Pathetic." My harsh, condescending words forced her mouth closed, her lips trembling.

"Fuck off, Enzo. Just because I wanted your dick doesn't mean that I like you. I don't have to like you to fuck you." Her words bit back at me, burning my skin as if she were spitting venom.

"You fucking bitch," I said, using my own poison against her. *Goddamn it, Gia.* I leaned into her, my lips so close to hers. Her chest heaved against mine.

"Fuck you," she hissed, but her anger deflated as she began to melt into the wall.

I fisted her hair, and she whimpered against my grasp. I dragged her toward the bedroom. She clawed at my wrists, trying to unleash my firm grasp.

"I'm gonna give you exactly what you want, Giovanna," I said as I tossed her onto the bed.

She rolled onto her back, her gaze entirely too calm for what I was about to do to her. I grabbed her hips, dragged her toward the end of the bed, and bunched her skirt at her hips, exposing her red panties. My fingers etched their marks into the soft skin of her thighs as I raked them downward. I grabbed her ass, lifting her hips as I leaned into her and kissed her. Her lips spread on mine with a fiery anger that was as hot as it was infuriating. Low moans rolled off her tongue. I worked open my jeans. Goosebumps pebbled her skin as the sound of my falling zipper hit the air. I pulled my cock out of my boxers, the hot skin of my hungry hands surrounding it. *Fuck,* I thought as the excitement fed an intoxicating level of desire. I was dripping for her as much as she was for me. Her lip trembled as she looked up at me. My hands trailed up her thighs and rubbed her pussy, making her jaw lax enough to let her moans escape them without impediment. She was soaked.

"Please," she begged.

Without another word, I pushed her panties aside and surged within her. She gasped as I forced every inch of myself inside. Her warmth surrounded me, tightening against me.

"Fuck," I groaned against her neck as I held myself within her for a moment, basking in her heat. It had been so long. Well, it felt like it, at least. She felt like home.

She looked up at me with a drunk expression, her head dropping back. I thrust harder and deeper, wanting her to take more of me than she ever had, until her moans mixed with the sounds of whimpers. I drove her into the mattress with my hips until I couldn't tell if she was whimpering from pain or pleasure, and I didn't fucking care.

She didn't tell me to slow down, let alone stop. Her nails dug into my back as I pounded her pussy. It took conscious effort to keep from busting too soon, and I wasn't ready for it to end. She arched her back, lifting her chest because of the pleasure I was drilling into and through her. She tightened around me, her thighs trembling.

"You know I ain't gonna let you come, right?" I raised an eyebrow, a sly grin on my face.

"I need you to, Enzo." She panted the words into the air.

"You only need to remember that you're mine," I growled into her neck before biting into her. "I'm going to fill you up and remind you who you belong to."

She flashed her eyes up at me, the depths dark enough to fall into. I started to pull out of her, to stop her from going over the cliff, but she fought me by wrapping her legs around me. She bucked against me, trying to come. I stopped, quieting the movement of my hips, and she let out a frustrated groan before sitting up on her elbows and biting her lip.

"Can we *please* not be enemies for one night?"

I smirked, leaning forward to kiss her. My lips clashed with hers, and I forced my tongue between them. I reached down and rubbed her as I let my hips resume their motion, albeit slower and deeper, feeling every squeeze of her as she moaned against my lips and trembled. She wrapped her arms around my neck and clung to me as she rode out her ascent. While she chased her pleasure, I let mine pour within her.

With a low growl against her neck, I said the only thing I could think of to describe the fucked up relationship between us.

"Goddamn it, Gia."

Chapter Thirty-Seven

Gia

We lay entwined at the hips, the heat of his spent cock against me. Our chests still heaved, a tangible remnant from our tryst. Enzo's head rested on the pillow, his blue eyes still dark with passion. My gaze roved over every curve of his chest and bare stomach. Our sweaty clothes lay on the floor. Sweat glistened on his tanned skin, each bead filled with desire.

"What?" he asked, his breath heavy with exhaustion.

"Nothing." I averted my gaze and turned onto my back.

"Babygirl, it ain't never nothing when it comes to you." He sat up on his elbow and wrapped an arm around my bare waist.

"I just miss my family," I said with heat teasing behind my eyes.

He brushed back my sweaty hair, his firm hand somehow still comforting. "I know."

"Can't I go back? No one knows about us or what

happened." I flashed my eyes at him, trying to hang on to the bit of hope I had left.

"Gia . . ." he began, shaking his head.

"I—"

"I said no!" He tensed, his arm squeezing around my waist.

"Why?" I pouted defiantly as I tried to push his arm away.

"I refuse to send you home where I can't protect you." He pulled me into him.

"Come with me?"

"Neither of us can show our faces in the city. Not now, at least. There's too many people who want us dead, and for good reason. Didn't you say you wanted out of that life?"

Of course I did. Well, I thought I wanted that. As scary as it was to be on guard and avoid the triggers of our enemies, there was also a sense of excitement. Something that I only got from danger and fucking. I imagined what kind of life we could have. Images of me perched on his lap while he ran his family flitted through my mind. Him fucking me with the power that could only come from running an empire with a Viglione and Silvani at the helm. If my intelligence coupled with his brutality, we'd be unstoppable.

"I said I wanted out of that life, yeah," I whispered.

"I know what you're thinking." He grabbed my chin and drew my face to him. "I've thought the same fucking thing, I'm sure."

"I just wish . . . I don't know . . . that we could run our own business. Maybe we aren't meant for this picket fence kind of life."

He kissed me, his tongue prying into my mouth and

igniting me again. "I've thought of that." He grinned. "Having you by my side, letting me fuck my stress out on you." Enzo reached down and grabbed himself. "I'm not even sure how much work we'd get done before my hands landed between your legs again."

His words made my entire body light on fire, and heat crawled beneath my skin. "Why can't we?"

"Because we can't run shit from outside the city." Enzo dropped his gaze. "We're out of this life, whether we like it or not. This picket fucking fence lifestyle is what we got now." He fisted my hair and pulled me into him, his lips hovering over mine. "But I can tell you this. I will make every fucking day we're here feel better than the last."

I knew he would. I wasn't sure it would be enough, but I was sure as fuck willing to try.

⌄

Enzo

I pulled Gia closer, and her pelvis pressed against mine. I hardened at the thought of her in a tight dress, leaning over my desk as my hands raced over her curves and she told me what business endeavors we should be in. *What a fantasy.* She looked at me with soft eyes filled with longing. I didn't know if I could give her what she wanted, but I could damn sure give her what she needed: out of the business. Death was a part of life for us, and we never got too attached to another person, not even family. I couldn't fathom the thought of losing her to some enemy over bullshit vendettas. Her deception was a catalyst to freeing us from that lifestyle, which meant it hadn't been a betrayal in the end.

Despite it all, there was still a nagging feeling in my gut where pain remained embedded in my tissue. "Gia . . ."

She turned toward me, her eyebrow cocked.

"Things happened to me as a kid, too. And it carried on for years."

She stared at me, motionless and silent. Shame began to well and boil in my veins. I was lying there, opening a big, raw wound where my secrets had chewed holes through my flesh.

"Oh, Enzo." She looked at me with sadness in her eyes that softened her features. She looked at me with pity, which I'd never wanted.

I got my retribution, and I came to terms with my pain. And by that, I meant I'd buried my feelings and tried to fuck and fight them away my entire life. My abuse made me unwilling to love another person, and I thought I was incapable of it. Gia had ignited things in me since we met all those years ago, when we fucked like we didn't hate each other. She created a smoldering fire within me, something that was not extinguishable no matter how much pussy I got. Gia didn't extinguish it, either. She made the fire roar and strengthen until it licked at my insides.

"I love you, even though you're a piece of shit Viglione." Gia leaned in and kissed me.

I grabbed her face and made her stop, unsure I'd heard that right. I definitely heard the piece of shit part right.

My heart thumped against my chest, pleading with me to say the words back. Words I'd thought about spilling before now. "I fucking love you, Giovanna Silvani." I pulled her into me and kissed her, letting my hunger for her drive my mouth.

We let ourselves become a wildfire, ripping apart every-thing in our path. With her, I never felt burned. But it was only a matter of time before our past would become a flame, hunting us down with its unbearable heat.

Closer to Sin

Book two, *Closer to Sin,* is available on Amazon. This book will finish up the Sin Duet, but not the world contained in these pages! Join my Patreon to be a part of polls and other reader input for this future world. Patreon.com/Lauren-BielAuthor. Join in on discussions in Lauren Biel's Trau-mances on Facebook.

Acknowledgments

A big thank you to my husband for sticking with me through this journey full of happiness, tears, and stress.

Some readers—my unicorns—have dried my tears when I felt like giving up. Christina, Sam, Kolleen, Terri, and most importantly, Ash, I love you all!

Thank you to my editor for working like a workhorse to help me get these books out. You're a superstar!

Connect with Lauren

Check out LaurenBiel.com to sign up for the newsletter and get VIP (free and first) access to Lauren's spicy novellas and other bonus content!

Join the group on Facebook to connect with other fans and to discuss the books with the author. Visit http://www.face book.com/groups/laurenbieltraumances for more!

Lauren is now on Patreon! Get access to even more content and sneak peeks at upcoming novels. Check it out at www.patreon.com/LaurenBielAuthor to learn more!

About the Author

Lauren Biel is an author with several titles in the works. When she's not working, she's writing. When she's not writing, she's spending time with her husband, her friends, or her pets. You might also find her on a horseback trail ride or sitting beside a waterfall in Upstate New York. When reading her work, expect the unexpected.

To be the first to know about her upcoming titles, please visit www.LaurenBiel.com.